CHOICE
OF THE
FALLEN

CHOICE OF THE FALLEN

ROBBIE AUGUST

INCENDIAT
www.incendiat.com

Published in the United States by Incendiat Press

ISBN-13: 978-1-7324072-1-3 (trade paper)
Library of Congress Control Number: 2018951813

First Edition: July 2018

Printed in the United States of America

0 9 8 7 6 5 4 3 2 1

to Jordan, for everything

CONTENTS

DARRAÐARLJOÐ

Vindum, vindum
vef Darraðar,
þars vé vaða
vígra manna;
látum eigi
líf hans farask,
eígu valkyrjur
vals of kosti

LAY OF DARTS

Let us wind, let us wind
the web of war
where the fierce
are forging forward;
we will not let
his life be lost,
only valkyries can
choose the slain

—*Stanza six, Njáls saga*

PART ONE

Γ

CHAPTER ONE

IN THE GREY LIGHT of an early northern dawn, a predator stalked her slumbering prey.

Aesa deftly navigated the dirty, melting snow piles that separated the settlement's footpaths from the glistening white expanse beyond. Seeing no one around her target's dwelling, she slid around the back of the low-roofed turf house. She worked the door bolt with chilly fingers then carefully eased the door open, trying not to let too many rays of the weak sunlight into the darkened space beyond.

A muffled noise came from the dimness, and Aesa froze, her fingertips gripping the doorframe in case she needed to fling it wide and dash through. The noise grew louder—was someone awakening? She hovered, uncertain, then relaxed as she identified the labored snore of a sleeper with a spring cold. Aesa crept forward on booted toes towards the slumbering form huddled for warmth on the far sleeping bench. She crouched over the prone body, smiling wickedly, leaning forward . . .

. . . and her intended victim's eyes opened. "You knocked the lock-stone against the door when you opened the bolt, and you smell like a corpse. Be stealthier next time, and I'll get to sleep that much longer," Ingirun said, squeezing her eyes shut again.

"I smell like Nidbiorg's very best scented oils," Aesa protested.

"A fresh corpse, then," Ingirun said. Aesa dropped onto the sleeping bench and snuggled into Ingirun.

After a silent interval, Aesa gently brushed the trim of her fur cloak against Ingirun's face. "Time to get up," she sang. Unsatisfied with the lack of results, she brushed faster. "Get up, get up, get up, get up."

"Any time now," Ingirun sing-songed. "I shall awaken. But not yet."

"Today is the day!" Aesa said, grimacing and batting at her friend's resisting body. "Sleep tomorrow!"

Ingirun just groaned.

"Some of us have to get there in time for a good place, since some of us weren't blessed with prior negotiations," Aesa said insistently.

"And some of us are trying to get more sleep after sending our husbands out early to complete those negotiations," complained an indistinct but aggrieved voice from further inside the deep gloom of the house.

"Sorry," Aesa called to the darkness apparently containing Ingirun's foster mother. She crouched by Ingirun again, lowering her voice to a whisper. "Aren't you worried about looking special for Porsi?"

"Porsi is being paid several sheep and who knows what all else so I do not have to worry about looking special for him," Ingirun said, and smiled a little. "But as one whose future very much relies on today, hadn't you better go?"

Aesa resorted to violent honesty. "If you don't come, I'll be left to face Sigrun by myself."

"Pish. You can handle Sigrun, and she'll have plenty of other targets on which to lavish her spite, so just go before she claims the best spot."

"There's a best spot?" asked Aesa, aghast.

"No, there isn't a best spot on Bride's Row," Ingirun said. "Haven't you been listening to anything we've been taught? There are just the bad spots—on the ends, and next to anyone with a better spread than you. Speaking of, I did not stay up with you all last night fixing your hemming just to let everything get overshadowed by Nefja and her ridiculous carvings, so shoo!"

"But . . ."

"Shooo! You'll be chosen, but not if no one can see you because you're blotted out by Nefja's glorious shade. I'll come down when I'm done hibernating. Shoooo." She rolled over, effectively ending the conversation. Aesa made a face at her friend's back, feeling sad and disappointed and suddenly wanting nothing more than to burrow down in the furs and ignore the future entirely.

Too much was riding on today, though, so she resettled her pack, slunk out of Ingirun's house, and padded down the path, sniffing at her wrist. She liked the juniper oils. She certainly didn't smell like a corpse, except maybe the funeral pyre bit.

She sniffed again, but now the smell of blood wafted into her nose along with the juniper scent. She glanced up, but quickly looked away when she spotted the source of the smell: sheep being carved up in the slaughter yard by large and boisterous butchers. The sheep would function both as traditional sacrifices to the gods and lunch at the great clan assembly.

This grubby mingling of the holy and ordinary upset her when she was younger. It clearly spoiled the magic. She'd complained once to her family, but her aunt had just laughed.

"We don't have enough sheep to feed the gods and those ravening hordes of elders," she'd said. "The gods won't mind a little bit of thrift."

Aesa hadn't been sure of that then and wasn't precisely sure now, but thinking about her family sent a wave of misery washing over her. She wished her father had made it back in time to see her, not to mention her mother. What sort of mother wasn't present today of all days?

Teasing shouts interrupted her gloomy reverie.

"Morning, Aesa," someone called out. "You look so worried. Can we help?"

Her sour expression must have caught the attention of one of the gore-spattered butchers.

She turned to smile politely, but had to look away again. She didn't know why the sight of the slaughtered animals sickened her so much, when she felt perfectly calm while tending the corpses of slain clansmen. But the sheep really were worse, somehow.

"Don't be so shy, Aesa," the biggest man, Gnupa, teased. "This is where your food comes from. Respect this sheep's gift to you, and look it in the face!" He picked up one of the severed, eyeless heads and made it nod at her in a chieftain's salute. The other butchers cracked up.

Aesa shuddered. "Why don't you do that further from the main road?" she grumbled, willing her feet to move faster.

"It's mortality, in all its glory. You should learn to deal with it." Gnupa gestured to the sheep he was gutting. "We warriors must. We know that this may happen to us any day, at the hand of our friends from across the river. You don't like me now, but think of how much you'll miss me when they step over my body and come for you."

He bared his teeth at her in a mocking grin.

The image of Gnupa's battle-corpse face—eyes wild but cold, face grey, that mocking grin turned to a rictus grimace—floated ghostly in her vision above the live face in front of her. Distracted, she didn't dodge when Gnupa flicked something across the path, and blood and guts spattered across the dirty snow.

Aesa shrieked in dismay, checking her clothing for red splashes, and Rodmar, another butcher, chimed in. "Don't fret, Aesa. If he's ruined your dress and no one picks you, I'll raise the bride ransom and marry you someday. You wouldn't be in thrall forever."

He licked the red, gory side of the sheep, staring at her and grinning. His companions snorted appreciatively, one near-doubled over with mirth.

Aesa bolted. The sound of the men's laughter floated after her, causing her to grimace at herself as she ran. She knew that by reacting to the men's teasing, she'd become an instant topic of their gossip. At least she hadn't snapped at them. Women who talked back were not lovable, and unlovable women were not chosen on Bride's Row.

Figures suddenly loomed up ahead of her, and she skidded to avoid running into someone's back. People, sleds, and animals now choked the packed-snow pathways. Aesa hissed in frustration. She'd tried so hard to be virtuously early, and now . . .

She tried hurrying through the deep snow piled on either side of the path, but floundered under the weight of her pack. A group of slap-happy striplings hauled her out again and volunteered to adopt her into their company. She declined their noisy offers with a smiling shake of her head, but her smile turned quickly into a grimace as she smacked her head soundly against the pommel of a poorly-stowed sword.

"Your face will stick that way, and then where will you be?" said a reedy voice at her shoulder. Aesa looked right to find her neighbor's son Sveni beaming cheerily at her over a wagonload of old wooden shields clearly destined for repair at the *þing* assembly.

"Still prettier than you, at least," Aesa said, nodding for emphasis. He laughed, but the movement caused the pile of shields to totter, so she quickly pushed the nearest stack further into the safety of the wagon. The rasp of wood sliding on metal-rimmed wood sparked an idea. She lifted the closest shield—a smooth, worn, oak disc, missing its spike—then looked from the snow-covered hill to Sveni's face, and grinned.

"Can I borrow one of these? Just for a few minutes?" Aesa asked.

Sveni's eyebrows knitted together. "Um, I s'pose?"

"If it doesn't survive, I'll pay you back." Aesa ignored Sveni's worried cries and darted to the side of the road. Squaring her shoulders, she burst into a full sprint and dove forward onto the shield, rocketing down the hillside. Snow sprayed behind her, while trees and rocks whizzed by her face as she clutched her makeshift sled's front edge. She really needed to do this again sometime, once she figured out how to steer.

But for now, there was nothing to do but enjoy the ride, and hope she didn't die.

The wise women would tell her that a good young woman would pray. Fine. "Óðinn, Freyja, Var and Elli, let your handmaid be all . . . whoops!" Aesa shrieked as she hit a rock near the bottom of the mountain, bounced hard, and flipped off the shield—which thankfully did not promptly thunk her in the head. She floundered in the snow for a moment, found some leverage, and managed to roll herself fairly gently down the last little bit of the foothill to the entrance of her final stop before the assembly: the grove of the gods.

On a normal day, upon entering the sacred space she would gaze upwards at the lacy intertwinings of the branches far overhead, and stop to appreciate the scale of the carefully-tended grove. This time, concern for the state of her clothing crowded out some of her awe. She leaned her shield against the roots of the closest tree and anxiously inspected her dress for marks. Her hem was damp, and a little soiled, but it would dry. Despite sounds of progress from the road filtering through the thicket, the vast tree-lined space was mostly quiet—almost eerily so. In the breeze, twig rattled against twig like bones in a corpse-cleaner's wagon. Shivering with nerves and chill, Aesa looked in vain for a friendly face among the early morning shadows. She was surprised more people weren't there in the circle of standing runestones, murmuring prayers for good sales or trades. But they weren't, so no one would chastise her for irreverent worship, if she was quick enough.

After an anxious glance at the position of the sun, Aesa untangled a knife from an inner pocket. A horn blast sounded from the *þing* proper, startling her such that she jabbed her finger much harder than she meant to. Staring at the welling blood for a moment in shock, she shook herself and touched the cut to each of the gods' representative stones, leaving behind yet another dark smear on surfaces already deeply stained. "Óðinn, Freyja, Var and Elli," she chanted quickly. "Eostre, Eir, Nanna, Sjǫfn." She skipped several names in the usually-beloved ritual, hoping that the gods of war and water would having nothing much to do with the proceedings, bit her lip, and bolted for the *þing*, shaking her still-bleeding hand.

There. She'd done everything she possibly could. Now her future was up to the gods, or, more probably, a bunch of cranky elders, and hopefully one in particular. Assuming, of course, that she didn't just trip and smash her face into something before she got there.

Dodging the last few loose stones on the path, she quickly glanced around and assumed a more decorous gait before covering the last few yards to her destination.

The *þing* assembly was held in a wide, flat meadow bordered by the sea. Aesa's village had been chosen to host it almost every time because such useful spaces were rare along their mountainous coast. Normally the site was only really remarkable for its *møtehall*—the large, low, dark building that huddled against the mountain in proper solemnity for a place of meeting and serious decision-making—but at some point some enterprising soul had realized he could make a fortune selling housewares to the bored, anxious women who crowded outside the building, waiting for the men of the district to filter out. Someone else had realized that men who left the *þing* were in a mood for active violence—either because of a planned raid, or because they were frustrated and tired of being cooped up. That someone brought armor merchants, and a fine-work blacksmith.

The outraged local blacksmiths started hauling their gear down the mountain and setting up temporary shops adjacent, to prove their mettle against the outsiders, and now the primary identifying feature of a *þing* was a joyfully cacophonous din, as monstrous anvils clanged and dozens of merchants screamed to be heard over them. People and animals roamed everywhere they could between stalls—barging about in a mostly-cheerful way and filling the valley with the mists of their cold breath.

The chaos meant that prospective brides who once stood demurely to the side of the meadow could no longer be easily seen by their prospective fathers-in-law. Some anxious mother or father had set up a large wooden pedestal near the *møtehall*, hoping to give their daughter a height advantage, and subsequently a permanent installation of stumpy carved platforms had sprouted along one whole side of the meadow.

Many of the nicest and least-wobbly stumps had been taken by the time Aesa got there. Contrary to Ingirun's insistence that there were no best spots, grumbling brothers were sometimes sent to camp overnight to protect a family's choice, so that sisters could arrive fresh-faced and as well rested as possible. Aesa hunched her shoulders a little as she searched for a gap in the wall of girls in fluttering dresses. Despite her best efforts, she briefly locked eyes with Sigrun, a pale-haired vision in expensive rose cloth. Sigrun smirked and tossed her head, and Aesa hurried on, trying not to worry. She'd never seen Kiaran speak to Sigrun. They probably weren't rivals. Not in this, at any rate.

Nearing one end of the row, she at last spotted a sunny space between Dotta, a local fisherman's daughter, and Geirny, the third child of a middle-ranked *karl*. The spot had likely been passed over because it was sunny, and would possibly cause her to squint, but Aesa didn't mind. Dotta and Geirny were both nice girls, and there likely would be no spitting or other attempts at last-minute social warfare. Aesa propped Sveni's shield against the stump, unrolled her embroidery and weaving samples, draped them over the top, then stood back to examine the effect. Perfectly acceptable. The great horn blew again, announcing the opening of the markets of all kinds.

"Is there a best way to get up on this thing?" Aesa asked as she scrambled about, trying not to knock her own display over.

"Don't trip," Dotta said, shrugging.

"All right, then."

Aesa set her knee on the pedestal, hoisted herself up, arranged her skirts, set her chin, and tried to look . . . prospective. But how did one look prospective? She snuck a glance at the faces on either side of her. Dotta and Geirny looked faintly nauseated. She'd fit right in.

All the preparation—the handiwork, the manners she'd been taught, and the outfit she was wearing—all of it led to this moment of total, frightening stillness. Her fate would be decided in the very next little while, and she could do little about it but look inviting and hope her efforts to be attractive were successful.

But really, what did success even look like? Her thoughts, unbidden, rattled down the list of possibilities. Marriage to a stranger, or even someone she found repulsive. Failure to attract an offer at all, and its resultant servitude or slavery. Well, probably not slavery. If her father returned before her funds ran out, he could likely find the money to keep her on in some capacity, if she could assert her value to him. Perhaps she could convince him to not spend quite so much of his coffers on keeping his armsmen loyal. She shook her head at herself, trying to plaster a pleasant expression back on her face. If she was picked by Kiaran's family, she'd become a *karl*—respectable and well-enough off with his father's farmstead, most seasons.

There would be the mystery of kissing to be solved. It looked nice, mostly. She thought Kiaran might know how to make it lovely. Below that secret hope of her heart lay a second, even more private: that as Kiaran's wife, she'd have a chance to make things here better.

As a kind of background constant her whole life, Aesa'd heard the screaming of harried mothers at their children, or the even more terrifying flinty and inescapable growls of the fathers, demanding to be obeyed. Those children were probably the ones who grew into the most callous warriors—unfeeling, brutish, and malicious to their captives. They were respected, in a way, but also brought so much danger to the community with their rages. And who could blame them? Who could stop it? Well, she could, perhaps. If she could raise a boy-child to be gentle, kind, and thoughtful, and hire the best tutors to make him into a fierce warrior, then her empowered son might rise up to be a *jarl* chieftain, and lead other men towards kindness and peace.

Or, if he was just strong, at least she might not become one of the grey-faced women whose failures littered the battlefield.

Her gaze flickered over the crowd again. Where was Kiaran's family? Wait, was he even there? Had Kiaran's mother looked at the crop of prospective brides and decided that no, it was not time yet to marry after all?

Admittedly, Kiaran had never actually said they planned to choose her. But when his mother had dropped hints about it being time for a bride, he'd always blushed and grinned right at her. He'd certainly never chased after anyone else too much. And he absolutely could have, for Kiaran was rather a handsome giant, even among the commonly tall and broad-shouldered men of their village. With his red-gold hair, he stood out like a fire against the dimness of the evenings. Maybe when he paid her bride-price, it would finally not be too forward to try to kiss him. *Or whomever chose her*, she corrected herself. Stupid, silly heart. She tried to find another prospective family in the crowd to smile encouragingly at. Geirny, on her left, suddenly sat down.

"Is that allowed?" a startled Aesa asked.

Geirny just rolled her eyes. "I'm tired. My feet hurt, and I'm near-promised to a kinsman from across the river who wants favorable terms from Father's connections. I'm just here because my father wanted to see if I might trade up before he agreed."

She glanced at a stern-looking woman standing near the front of the crowd who was making tiny but furious gestures, and reluctantly stood up again. "So who've you been courting?"

"No one."

"Aesa, we're on the pedestals, and I'm bored and annoyed. Please entertain me. You don't have to worry about my stealing him now, so you can tell me."

Aesa glanced at Geirny with a little suspicion, but realized unburdening herself might help her calm down. "Well, Kiaran, I suppose, but I haven't been courting him." It felt strange saying his name aloud. She'd only even whispered of her crush to Ingirun.

Geirny looked unimpressed by her boldness, though. "Silly, you're supposed to pursue him, to show him what a good wife you'd be."

"I mean, I tried, I suppose. They were just always so busy at the farm—and Gnorri, his mother, always complains if a village woman so much as throws a glance in his direction. So I stayed out of the way when I visited, and didn't hang all over him at dances. I was quiet, and polite, and respectful. Oh, and I tried magic, of course. I did all the chants, and got Ingirun to make the sacrifices to Freyja for me."

Geirny stared at her. "And you thought that would work?"

"Well, yes," Aesa said. To Geirny's amazed-looking face, she said defensively: "It's what we've been taught."

"Well, sure," Geirny almost spat. "But didn't your mother explain that . . ." Her face went ashen as realization dawned. "No, your mother is your mother, so she didn't."

"Explain what?" Aesa asked, her heart sinking.

"Darling, the wise women are full of it. Nothing they teach us about men works. It's never worked. Men just like to be fed, and to see women in the all-together, and to have good help on the farm. That's mostly all it takes. I'm so sorry you didn't know."

Frustration and anxiety roiled in Aesa's stomach. "But they schooled us for years!"

"Right, because they get shirty admitting how they keep their men, and they'd rather pretend to something more genteel. And the housekeeping knowledge is generally good, at least. The mystical bits, though . . ." Geirny broke off and shook her head. "I'm so sorry. I would have said something if I'd known."

Aesa bit her lip, and looked out over the staring crowd. It didn't matter. Kiaran's father was going to be there. He would be there, or there would be someone else—someone who wasn't churlish, or blood-mad. None of the few men milling near the Bride's Row looked terribly fearsome, although several of them were strangers. Some were a little furtive, and glanced back and away at the women as though they'd be caught. She supposed they could just be shy, or embarrassed to be seen contemplating domesticity. She put on her biggest smile and tried to look approachable. It would be all right. It would. She would make it all right. Rodmar the butcher might be prevailed upon to marry her. He was a boisterous, jolly man, often, and not too much like Gnupa. But . . .

There. She caught her breath. There it was—the white head of Kiaran's father, Vigi Ulfrikson! Her brief, joyous surge of relief quickly faded as she realized that Vigi was involved in an arm-waving conversation with Dotta's father. Reflexively, a prayer started up in Aesa's head. *Óðinn the All-Father, let that argument be about a sporting match and not Dotta's bride price. . . .*

She frowned at herself. She should wish the best for Dotta. But really, with their fishing enterprise, Dotta's family could afford to keep her if necessary. She would not become a thrall bondswoman, slaving in another's household until the debt she incurred by merely existing was somehow considered paid. If it ever could be. Aesa had heard of thrall men buying their way out of the bond and setting up somewhere else, but never a lone woman. It would be too dangerous.

Without admitting it to herself, she'd put all of her eggs in Kiaran's basket. Now she might pay dearly for her folly. She smiled frantically at a stranger, who looked away, clearly discomfited. In her shame, it struck her with force that Dotta and Geirny, ramrod straight on either side of her, were not only good and kind and skilled but also completely unobjectionable, whereas she did wild things like steal people's shields and go hurtling down the mountainside on them. . . .

Aesa tossed her head, trying to halt her runaway worries. Stop thinking of your rivals, she told herself. Stop thinking of dignified fathers and clucking mothers. Look over the heads of this crowd. Imagine being able to summon your totem *fylgia*, the giant snow bear. It could eat them all if you wanted it to.

Look at the beautiful treeline and the slopes of the forested mountainside, and the path that carves down the foothills like a dusty river. Do not look at Vigi. Don't think of demure Dotta's big eyes compared to yours, or Geirny's even temper, or wish for unique, raven-black hair like . . .

Ingirun's! Ingirun was here!

Aesa nearly clapped her hands for joy as she watched her dark-haired friend pick her way through the crowd on the trail. Ingirun had come after all, and would make faces and roll her eyes at everyone, and give Aesa something besides impending doom to focus on. Aesa wasn't alone. Look, Ingirun was even coming to the very front of Bride's Row. She was . . . steadily looking away from Aesa's beseeching gaze. Ingirun . . . was setting out the holy symbols and implements of her healing skills onto a vacated pedestal. Aesa leaned out, trying to get a better view, until Dotta tugged on the right side of her skirt. After a glance at the mute plea for decorum on Dotta's face, Aesa forced herself to settle back.

Robbed of her view of Ingirun's proceedings, Aesa instead stared at the treeline as though it had burst into flames. Why hadn't Ingirun said anything about her plans? Thanks to her foster-father's efforts that morning, she was practically betrothed to Porsi. She shouldn't be standing in this village's Bride's Row at all, since she'd only been sponsored by her wealthy family to come here and learn the secrets of wound-tending from a Bjǫrn clan foster-mother. Aesa saw Kiaran's father move deliberately in Ingirun's direction. No, he couldn't. . . . Incredulous, Aesa searched for memories of Kiaran and Ingirun's interactions. She recalled so few. She was fairly sure neither had demonstrated a particular affection, beyond Kiaran's generic flirting. Had they met in private? Was there an agreement of some kind? But how could there be? Aesa rarely spoke of Kiaran, but when she did, it was to Ingirun. She'd been grateful for Ingirun's silent, patient listening then. Had Ingirun's silence actually masked her own feelings?

Fingers of cold crawled over Aesa's body. Frantic with worry, she leaned out again. Dotta coughed meaningfully, but Aesa's surroundings faded into a fuzzy haze as she tried to focus on events down the row. Ingirun was bowing to Vigi, and he smiled as he bowed back. Now he was turning—leaving—with all the other men, as a horn blew again to call the important business of the *ping* to order. He did not look back.

"Ingirun," Aesa hissed. She tried again, more loudly. "Ingirun!"

Ingirun refused to turn her head, and Dotta, unfortunate in her proximity, winced at Aesa's volume. "We're not supposed to shout," she reminded Aesa, rubbing her ear.

"I know," Aesa said with a wince. "It's just that . . ."

"Shh," Geirny said, from the corner of her mouth. "Your man's coming." And, praise all of the gods, she was right. There was Kiaran, headed towards her through the throng of men streaming the other way, and smiling. Aesa felt herself smile back reflexively, and took a deep breath.

"Hullo, nubbin," he said, his voice ringing cheerfully through the emptying space. "How's business?"

Aesa felt her nose wrinkle at his apparent unconcern. "Fine?" she managed at last.

He grinned at her consternation. "What's to say you reclaim your dignity and come with me on an adventure?"

"An adventure?"

"Yeah, unless you'd rather hang 'round here with this lot," he said, winking at Geirny. "No offense."

Geirny rolled her eyes at him.

Aesa looked worriedly around the clearing, but Kiaran tugged at her hem. "Don't worry, I'll have you back before the end of the meeting part of the *ping*, so none of the eligible bachelors holed up in the hall will miss out." He held out his hand then, and she found herself clasping it, and stepping down off the stump.

Go, something inside her said, and suddenly bright and joyful as she'd ever been, Aesa laughed at her own daring.

"Hold my place?" she said to Geirny, who smiled and nodded.

But instead of leading her away, Kiaran escorted her by the elbow down the row of women. "Ingirun's had the capital idea of investigating that haunted burial cave to see if we can find some haunted treasure," he said, nodding to Ingirun herself, who had appeared at Kiaran's other side and tucked her arm through his. "I thought you wouldn't want to miss out."

Aesa missed a step as her heart froze at the sight of her betrayer. "But it's forbidden. And probably disgusting. And why today of all days?" she asked irritably, hauling herself fully upright again.

"Because no one will be watching it, silly," Ingirun said, smiling sweetly into Aesa's dismayed face. "There's usually a lookout stationed up there. He'll be at the *ping* today. But I understand if you don't want to come."

Strange motes danced in Aesa's vision, nearly obscuring the sight of her former friend. "I want to come," Aesa said, her tongue feeling thick in her mouth. "I want to come," she said again, glancing from Kiaran to Ingirun to make sure she'd been heard. Looking at Ingirun burned her eyes, somehow, and she turned away again. Some part of Aesa was amazed at how quickly her affection turned to fury, but while the Ingirun of five minutes ago had been a treasured confidante, the woman now standing front of her was making a play to destroy Aesa's most cherished dreams. Aesa felt the prick of oncoming tears.

"Let's go," she said firmly, and set off before anyone noticed the tell-tale glisten in her eyes.

Ϝ

CHAPTER TWO

As THE THREESOME ARRIVED at the edge of the broad clearing, Ingirun glanced over her shoulder at the low-roofed *møtehall* that by now contained all of the men of the clan excepting the truant Kiaran. Then, with a conspiratorial wink, she ducked under some branches to pull Kiaran onto the tree-bounded dirt of a little-used game track.

Aesa pushed a stray bough away from her head, impressed that enemy-Ingirun had resisted the urge to drop the branches back into her face after Kiaran passed under them. On second thought, Ingirun was too clever to let outright hostility push him toward Aesa.

It was to be a smiling sort of fight, then. Time to arm up.

She crouched, pulling at a snowdrop that'd had the misfortune to bloom early and tucking it behind it behind Kiaran's ear.

When he looked down at her, she beamed a brilliant smile full into his face. His grin widened. "Keep up," he said, increasing his stride and tugging both women by their elbows.

"Of course," said Ingirun. "We've got to get this little one back to her place."

"And you," Aesa said. "Your intended might change his mind if he doesn't think you care enough to wait for him." She'd no idea if Porsi was at the *ping* or not, but she could see that her strike had hit home.

Ingirun smoothed the rage out of her face as Kiaran lifted an eyebrow at her.

"That agreement isn't as final as Porsi thinks it is," she said stiffly. Aesa longed to find out more, but she knew that to ask in front of Kiaran would be combative. She refused to stoop to Ingirun's level of unkindness. Aesa risked a glance across Kiaran's chest at her former friend. Perhaps Ingirun was actually being practical and wise in her ruthlessness, and she herself was a dreamy-hearted idiot.

The technical demands of navigating a series of ice-coated boulders forced her thoughts to the trail again, and so they clambered up the mountainside, Aesa all fierce smiles and furtive unhappiness, until they reached a mist-shrouded crack in the rock. The dark mouth of the cave seemed to gape gloomily at the bright, festival atmosphere below. Aesa shivered.

"Cold?" Kiaran pulled her solicitously closer.

"She's just playing scared," Ingirun said. "Come off it, lovey, we know you're game. Or would you rather stand guard while Kiaran and I explore?"

Aesa took a step toward the cave. The light outlining the mountain peaks just served to make the rune-carved entrance even darker somehow. It had been easy to ignore their destination on the trek up, surrounded by sun-bright snow and early birdsong, but now it repelled her. She couldn't remember why, precisely, the burial cave had been spell-sealed and forbidden by the village wise women. Staring straight at the cavern, though, her imagination could invent all kinds of reasons.

Were those shapes shifting within its pathways, or just shadows?

"There are probably bears," she said, shrugging nonchalantly.

"Bears!" Ingirun scoffed. "It's too early for bears."

"Exactly," Aesa said. "They're probably still sleeping, and I've already woken one vicious bear up today."

Kiaran coughed into the following silence.

"If there are bears, I will defend you," he said. "Bears fear me. Rawr."

Aesa stuck her tongue out at him, but could not shake the feeling of chill emanating from the cave entrance. "Defend Ingirun. I'll guard your retreat, from right here."

"You're such a good girl, Aesa," Ingirun said, her smile a mixture of triumph, pity, and disgust.

"And you aren't?" Aesa shot back.

"Sometimes," Ingirun said, shifting her smile to Kiaran.

Aesa fought down a gagging noise. Ingirun must have figured that Aesa, so often awkward and shy, would not—could not—compete seductively. Deep down, she feared that Kiaran would think less of her if she even tried. Resolute but grim, she turned her back on the pair and took a seat against the cool stone. She didn't watch as the other two slipped into the caverns behind her. Trying to beat back the waves of anxiety that threatened to overwhelm her, she focused with furious intensity on the vistas of the white-rimmed valley spread out below. To her great surprise, the view did slightly soothe her heartache. A playful breeze brushed sparkling snow from the top of the ridges, and the bright flags of the *ping* stood out in amusingly toy-like contrast to the dark crags and sheer slopes of the mountains around them. If it hadn't been such a sunny day, the fires of the blacksmiths would have been particularly striking.

Except something bothered her about the flames below.

All the blacksmiths should have closed up shop and gone to the *møtehall*. There shouldn't have been any fires going. Especially not one so bright, and fierce, and large, and against that side of the mountain . . .

The scream tore from Aesa's throat before she could think about forming it. Behind her, Kiaran shouted questions, but her horror robbed her of further breath, and she could only point insistently at the flames licking at the council hall. Kiaran arrived at her side, but almost immediately halted. *He must not see the fire.* She began to run towards the village, but found the air choked out of her lungs as Kiaran caught her around the middle, stabbing a frantic finger over Aesa's shoulder until she registered a second deadly light source: glints of sun flashing from countless enemy blades. Undaunted, she tried to press on, but Kiaran restrained her struggling form until her fury pulled them both off balance and they fell to the ground.

"There's too many," Kiaran hissed, stifling her protests with his hand. "Don't draw attention."

Aesa considered biting him, but Ingirun plucked urgently at their sleeves. "Her dress is bright like a beacon. They'll see us," she said. "We've got to get into cover."

"We can help people escape, at the least," Aesa said, but Kiaran hauled her back up the hill and into the dimness of the cave anyway. Her hands clutched reflexively at the carvings etched in its rough stone as she passed them, but they offered no purchase, and she found herself dumped somewhat unceremoniously onto the floor of a chill, grey emptiness. Outraged, she made a scrambling break for the door. Kiaran blocked the cave mouth with his body and settled his weight into a wrestler's stance.

"Let me out," Aesa demanded, scanning his pose for points of potential attack.

Kiaran shook his head. "It's my job right now to keep us safe."

Aesa felt her face contort with incredulity. "What about everyone else?"

Backlit as he was, Aesa couldn't really make out his expression, but his voice sounded grim and sorrowful. "Strategically speaking, our best option is stay put."

"Protect Ingirun, then, but let me go."

Kiaran shook his head. "I couldn't live without both of my girls. You know that, right?"

Aesa looked to Ingirun for support, but the other woman gazed steadily at her.

"We're not going anywhere right now, Aesa," she said. "It would save us some trouble if you'd accept that."

Aesa flopped to the stone floor in exasperation. Her eye was drawn to an elaborate pattern etched across the ceiling of the cave— the grotesque shapes made more eerie by the limited light filtering around Kiaran's form.

"Ugh, this is what you wanted to see?" Aesa said to Ingirun, gesturing toward the depictions of bloody hunts and ritual sacrifice. "We've probably upset some spirit or god or something by intruding here. We should go while we can."

Ingirun made a face. "There are no gods except those you believe in," she said. "Believe they won't eat you, and they probably won't."

"But . . ."

"There are no bears either," Ingirun said. "The cave gets too narrow for a bear to fit. Now be quiet. We need to think."

Aesa glanced at Kiaran, but he only gazed out at the valley, his face unreadable. "We don't need to think," she hissed. "We need to *go*. We could still save people."

"No, *we* cannot," Ingirun said fiercely. "You saw the enemy's strength. Even if you didn't, *I* did. We are outnumbered and un-armed and we will only add our own corpses to the pile." Aesa rose to look for herself again, but Kiaran seized one of her arms as she tried to push past him.

"At best they will enslave you," Ingirun said. "Or maybe at worst, I don't know. But I do know that I am not letting you out of here to give away my position while I still have a chance. We'll go down when those men are gone, and I will see what I can do if there are survivors. But in the meantime, we will wait."

She stared into Aesa's face intently for a moment, then got up and moved further out of the light. "Kiaran, sit on her if you have to," she said over her shoulder.

"With pleasure," he started to say, then winced. "Sorry," he said more quietly. "I'm a little punchy right now. My father's down there, and . . ." He shook his head, and fell silent.

Aesa longed to say that this was even more reason for them to see what good they might do against the invaders, but respect for Kiaran's mourning stilled her tongue.

It was Ingirun who broke the silence. "If your father dies in battle, then he dies with the greatest honor. Is there more that any of us could want of our fate?"

"Your father is brave and mighty. One of the war gods will surely claim him for their own," Aesa added, anxiously searching Kiaran's face for a sign that they had brought him some comfort.

Kiaran's expression did not change, but Ingirun gazed at Aesa for a long moment. At last she sighed and leaned back against the cave wall, sinking along its cold support until she could rest her forehead on her knees.

Aesa looked from Ingirun to Kiaran again. She could not read much in his half-lit face, but she thought she saw both determination and fear in his normally cheerful eyes. Sadness suddenly sapped her limbs of energy. She could not risk those who were with her, and Ingirun was right: unarmed and unskilled, there was little she could do to help those below. The grief of her uselessness overwhelmed her, and she settled into a despondent crouch against the edge of the cave mouth, gazing out at the stricken village.

Their shadows grew long and cold seeped into their stiffened joints, but the three did not move or speak again until the inky black smoke rising from the fires mixed with the deepening gloom of nightfall.

F

IN HINDSIGHT, it wasn't the best decision. What might have been bleak but tolerable in daylight was by night an ember-lit landscape of loss and horror. The three stood at the edge of the smoking ruins, arms folded as though to put a sort of barrier between them and what lay ahead. Considering the circumstances in which they lived, Aesa thought, the wise women really ought to have taught a lesson called "What to Do if You're the Survivor of a Raid." She supposed it would be an affront to the pride of the clan—to admit they could ever be raided in turn.

Ingirun squared her shoulders and set off towards the *møtehall*. Aesa followed quickly—of course, they would do their battlefield duties. Everything was all simple after all.

But there was no need for Ingirun's skills there in the ruins, nor Aesa's. The raiders had been methodical—kind, in a way—for no one had been left to suffocate, or burn alive. Stripped of their ostentatious, *þing*-day finery and wealth, the men here had all been professionally dispatched. The raiders obviously hadn't wanted to leave competent fighters behind to rally other clans and seek revenge.

Women *could* plead for aid, of course, and sometimes one or two had actually stumbled, ragged and haunted and furious, into Aesa's rather remote mountain clan village. But whatever kind of kinship might stand between the great clans was, for whatever reason, not often roused by a woman's voice. Instead the chieftains of Aesa's clan had shaken their heads, patted the women gently on their shoulders, and recommended they find some house where they might live in service.

"The men must be mindful of the clan's well being," Aesa's mother said when appealed to. But once Aesa had seen a petitioning war-band arrive, banging on their shields and shouting, to which Aesa's father himself had roared a welcome. There had been much clapping of shoulders and backs, after which the clan had risen up and ridden out to a great pitched battle, followed by a celebratory feast. She shook her head at the contrast between the memory and the bleak view before her now. They'd need to look to themselves for help.

For outside the meeting hall, circumstances were much the same. The raiders had, either short-sightedly or in a berserker rage, killed craftsman and clansman alike. When word got out they would no doubt feel the consequences of traders not wanting to venture near their lands.

In the mean time, though, Ingirun and Kiaran struggled to find a soul to help. They paced methodically across the clearing, shouting to be heard above the crackles and retorts of the dying flames, but no one answered.

Aesa looked towards Bride's Row, her heart in her mouth, but it was empty of bodies. The sight was still bleak—the pedestals that had so recently contained a sunlit bevy of hopeful women now re-minded Aesa of the gap-toothed grin of a forgotten battlefield skull. The once-brave work displays had been ransacked for treasure, but since the raiders had apparently not correctly calculated the trade value of the fancywork, most of them had simply been knocked over, and their goods remained largely intact.

Intact . . . the ground itself was too intact. Aesa hurried over to the row of pedestals to get a closer look. There she found the marks of a hundred booted feet, both from the morning festival and the afternoon's terrible events, no doubt. But there was no sign of protest—no blood, no deep impression from a man carrying a weight over his shoulder, and no furrows created by protesting, struggling feet. What she did see was a multitude of broken branches in the rough hedges behind the stands.

Hope surged in her chest. Someone might have broken through, and even gotten away. She shouted joyfully to Kiaran and Ingirun. Without waiting for a response, she charged into the bushes, batting frantically at the twigs that yanked at her hair and clothes. On the other side, a loose scree of rocks at the foot of the mountain slopes hid any tracks, but to those who lived in this area, the foothills were familiar as friends. And every native child knew that the best place to hide from a parent calling them home was around this part of the mountain, to a cranny out of view from all the village houses, even the ones on the other foothills. . . .

"It's me! It's Aesa! You're safe!" she started calling before she came around the bend, and sure enough, as she cleared the turn and stopped to catch her breath again, she spotted her reward: a large group of huddled forms, their faces scared and dirty, but alive.

The shadowy twilight made them appear fey and unfamiliar, but Aesa still picked out Geirny, Dotta, and Nefja, at least. So many faces, but still so few. She fought back her tears and went to work.

"Any sign of Sveni?" she asked Geirny as they helped to extract the others from their rocky hiding place. Geirny bit her lip.

"I think he may have been captured, along with my mother and Ingirun's foster," Geirny said. "I could only get the women from the Row."

Aesa nodded, sad and grim. "Do we know who they were?"

"Skjöldungar, I think," said Nefja, huffing a little as she hauled herself up the slope. "Not the main branch—one of the feral cadets. Their totems were weird. How bad is it at home?"

Her tone was light, but her eyes were hungry. Aesa had to look away.

"It's bad. I don't think they headed up the slopes to the township proper, but if you have menfolk, be prepared for . . ." Aesa trailed off, unsure of the words to use.

Geirny nodded. "We know. We saw enough," she said, and started back towards their home. The women trailed slowly behind her across the murky landscape—either less certain about their footing in the dimness, or not entirely sure if they really wished to arrive.

When they got closer, the group shied a little, for a new, bright flicker was playing off of the shadowy chaos of the valley. By some unspoken decision, Dotta and Nefja gathered and stilled the main body while Aesa and Geirny crept forward, trying to stay near cover.

As they reached the edge of Bride's Row, Geirny suddenly stiffened. She squinted. To Aesa's touch of inquiry, she said in a low voice, "I think that might be help."

Straightening and brushing themselves off, the two approached the group of torch-bearing men inspecting the wreckage of the *þing*. Strangers to Aesa's eyes, they bore totems of the wolf scattered about their clothing—clothing that was too fine for raiding, although they were heavily armed, nonetheless. Aesa quickly glanced around the area, but saw no obvious sign of Kiaran or Ingirun. Perhaps they'd hidden at the strangers' approach.

Aesa accidentally kicked a loose pebble, and the men tensed, laying large hands on larger weapons. Geirny raised a hand in a sort of salute, and one of the men relaxed and hurried forward. "You're all right," the man said wonderingly, looking first at her, then at the destruction all about them. He blushed suddenly—a startling bloom of color on a face so pale. "Er, I mean, hail, Geirny Róghvatrsdóttir of the Bjørning."

"Greetings, Jófreiðr of the Ylfings," Geirny said, inclining her head slightly. "It's kind of you, but I don't think we need stand on ceremony right now."

"Yes, well," Jófreiðr said, a little awkwardly. "Is this, um, all of you? We haven't found anyone else." He glanced at Aesa, who tried to look reassuring.

"I'm not going to faint, or anything," she said. "I've assisted at clan battles before. Have your men searched beyond this area? Our houses are mostly up in the foothills."

He brightened at this, and shook his head. "We were coming for the evening part of the *þing*, to do the formal clan introductions, and we've mostly only had time to look through your gathering hall. I'm sorry there's not more to be done there," he said, looking back over his shoulder at the smoldering ruin. "We'll send our squad up, let your people know it's all right to come out."

"No, we'll do that," Aesa said. "Your men will look like enemies in the dark, and we don't want any of them attacked by someone feeling brave. Also, we need you to go after our families. The Skjöldungar took prisoners."

Jófreiðr winced; then Aesa watched an unnameable expression flicker across his face. "Well," he said slowly, "we're not a fighting force. And these things take time, you know. Are you sure it was the Skjöldungar? It's so dark, it could have . . ."

"It wasn't dark then," Geirny said firmly. "And they have my mother."

"Yes, well," Jófreiðr said again, "this squad isn't really my command, not formally. But I'll see what I can do." He turned to walk away, then stopped. "Keep your spirits up," he said. "It'll all come out all right."

"Maybe you could take Geirny back with you," Aesa said, suddenly. "To keep her safe, you know." She stopped in some confusion when Geirny glared daggers at her, and Jófreiðr looked at her in consternation.

"Thank you," Geirny said, with some asperity. "But I must stay here, since I have our family's livestock to care for." She and Jófreiðr took a formal leave, with promises to return tomorrow, while Aesa twisted her skirts between her fingers. Of course there were firm notions about chaperoned travel for their caste, but surely this once the rules could be broken, since they were defenseless? Surely someone else could care for Geirny's dratted cows?

As Jófreiðr walked away, Aesa turned to apologize for butting in, only to discover that Geirny was not shocked, but seething.

"I'm sorry I suggested it without consulting you," Aesa said, "but you needn't be so angry with me. It's bound to be safer with them."

"Safer for whom? Maybe them, honestly. That man won't even agree to rescue his near-betrothed's mother; how brave can he possibly be? I'm not angry at you, I'm furious at this milksop politicking."

"Politicking?"

"The Ylfings want to rule the Geats. Did you see how Jófreiðr flinched when I told him who attacked us? That probably means the Ylfings are cultivating the Skjöldungar for support, and Jófreiðr won't risk a potential alliance by pursuing them. Or even if that marshmallow would, his uncle certainly won't let him, even if it's the right thing to do." Geirny spat into the dirt.

Aesa sucked a breath through her anxiously-constricted chest, but Jófreiðr and his men had by this time cast off, and could just be made out as darker shapes against the darkness of the water.

"I suppose we should go see what's been left us," Aesa said, after a moment's grim silence. Many of their companions had already climbed the hill that led to the village residences, and lights were beginning to show themselves at windows.

"I'm going to the pastures to make sure our livestock is still in fact ours," Geirny said. "Find me later if you want company."

Aesa nodded, and touched Geirny's shoulder as she walked away. She thought briefly of trying to find Kiaran, but shuddered when her traitorous imagination conjured up a picture of him finding comfort in Ingirun's arms.

Hiking up the long slope to her home, Aesa's sense of aloneness increased, as she witnessed many reunions in progress. It seemed as though these houses had not been touched in the raiders' hasty smash-and-grab, and anyone who had not been at the *þing* had been wise enough to stay put. Their losses were still palpable and grievous—everywhere she looked, she saw the faces of old women, and very young children, but there were no men left who could wield an axe. Everyone had lost fathers or brothers or husbands. Even the likes of Gnupa had gone to the *þing* to enjoy their day of male camaraderie and equality. And beyond their personal tragedy loomed the fact that if word got out, and another raiding party descended like crows on a carcass . . .

She shook her head. That was a problem for tomorrow. Tonight's remaining problems were now, suddenly and strangely, the same as always—heat, a solitary dinner, and trying to sleep in the cavernous home that was meant for a whole family, but contained only her.

But who knew? Perhaps tomorrow her parents might finally return.

CHAPTER FOUR

By the time the sun's light had overcome the mountain's shadow the next day, neither Aesa's family nor Jófreiðr had yet arrived. Aesa spent the morning cleaning fish on the village shore and keeping a hopeful lookout. It was full noon when a solitary boat touched the pebbly sand of their beach, towed in by a thin thrall who, from the look of him, likely had been captured from the skraeling people to the west. The man who clambered ashore with the thrall's assistance was not Jófreiðr. Instead, a man Aesa thought might have been in Jófreiðr's retinue looked about himself, clearly uncertain of how to proceed. Aesa, Geirny, and several other women rose from their tasks to meet him.

He skimmed a glance over them, then looked hopefully over their shoulders. "Hail, women of Bjǫrning," he said, shaking his wet feet. "Might you bring me to your chieftains for discourse?"

"We have no chieftains currently among us," Geirny said. "You may speak to their wives."

"Ah," said the hapless warrior. "Are there *karlar* men available, then? A high-ranking farmer, perhaps?"

"Despite the tragedy yesterday, our clan is busy at their planting, as yours must be," Aesa said. "It will take some time to summon them. Perhaps you can relate your message to us. You were sent by Jófreiðr for us, were you not?"

His gaze flickered anxiously over their faces again. "Protocol, and all that. You understand," he said hazily. "I will happily wait." The resigned face of the thrall somewhat belied this sentiment.

"Um," Aesa said. "Of course," Geirny said, and nudged Aesa with her elbow. When Geirny turned and started up the hill, Aesa followed her, doing her best to appear demure and calm, until they were over the rise and solidly out of both sightline and earshot.

"Can you get Kiaran to come?" Geirny hissed urgently. "Probably," Aesa said, eyes shifting. "If someone wants to find him."

"Lost track of your man, have you?"

"Things are . . . more complicated than I thought," Aesa admitted. "If nothing else, we can ask Ingirun to ask him."

"Ah," said Geirny, making a face.

"But that warrior was here last night. He's probably already guessed about the state of our clan, and if he hasn't, someone in his squadron will likely be making those guesses out loud across the river anyway. I thought we should hide it, but now I'm not sure if it's worth trying. Maybe we should try the opposite tack—do a big show about how we're poor, deprived women, and send him back to Jófreiðr with a brimming heart."

"Well, we are poor, deprived women," Geirny said. "From what I've heard, our men had most of their wealth on their persons. I think someone was trying to scrape together funds to hire a mercenary warband, but she hasn't had much success."

"Well, there you go. We're destitute, so we should, I don't know, snivel, or something."

"You snivel. I'm going to try haughty princess."

"Or maybe by the time we get back, Dotta will have magically sorted the whole thing, and an army of liegemen swearing fealty will have landed on our shore."

This proved, sadly, not to be the case. The warrior and his thrall had settled uneasily on a stump near the wreckage of the *møtehall*, and were watching Dotta and the others work in the ruin. The warrior's face was bright red, and his lips were tight, as though some exchange had gone poorly.

Geirny caught his eye as they approached, and inclined her head. "Thank you for your patience," she said. "I've sent runners to the far villages, but I fear your message will not be sweeter with age. Will you not entrust me with it, so you may return to your own weighty business?"

"I'm glad to know there's someone to speak to at all," he said. "I'm concerned about all this, you know," he continued, gesturing to the women in the wreckage. "While the honor they do to your dead does them credit, I think it, ah, unsafe."

"We would not leave it to our servants to handle our family," Geirny said. "As I'm sure you understand. Your concern and your discretion are admirable. We Bjørn women have served many times on the battlefield in just such a manner."

"Yes, well, that *møtehall* doesn't look quite stable. Ought to be torn down."

"Indeed," Geirny said, her mouth tightening a little. "Highly unsafe. But your message, sir—will you let me have it?"

The warrior turned to Geirny, and Aesa watched as his gaze flicked over her, clearly looking for the hallmarks of status. Seemingly satisfied, he shrugged in resignation.

"Your fathers would no doubt understand what to you may seem ungallant," he said, fixing his eyes into the middle distance over Geirny's shoulder. "Jófreiðr and his family do not think it prudent at this time to make any, well, let us say 'unresearched accusations.' The honor of the Bjǫrning is of course dear to them, as it is to all of us, and they are prepared to offer you and your remaining clan shelter, and to send slaves to till your fields, with commensurate reward in the harvest, of course."

"They want to annex us," Aesa snarled, rage claiming her tongue. "You don't offer help, but ownership."

Her eyes locked on the warrior's appalled face, Geirny said smoothly, "The plan is unsurprising in its generosity—everything I'd expect from the Ylfing. We are not without recourse or protection, however. The planting is well underway, and we expect the return of several warbands of our finest men to our shore at any time. Aesa's father, one of our great chieftains, for instance, will likely become our leader, and we must naturally wait to accept Jófreiðr's offer until his counsel has been sought. I think it likely, however, that your kindness will not, in fact, prove necessary."

"Ah," the warrior said. "Excellent. In the meantime, however, I know that Jófreiðr and his family will fear for your well-being when I give them my report of your situation. You are . . . exposed, in a way that your fathers could not like. While the warriors with you are no doubt fearsome and doughty, in the way of all Bjǫrning, their strength cannot hope to stand against a second assault, were others to learn of your, ah, predicament."

The words sounded as threatening to Aesa as the rasp of a blade against its scabbard.

"But we, as kinsmen, know well of the likely demands on your clan as well," she said brightly, trying to mimic Geirny's formal meter. "Surely your menfolk do not sit idly, or look far for tasks for their energy. Mighty though they are, we could not ask you to sacrifice the safety of your own families for what remains of ours by stretching your defenses too thinly. So our warriors here plan to teach us to fight . . . er, defend ourselves," she amended, looking from the warrior's shocked face to Geirny's surprised one in some trepidation.

Geirny urgently began to cover. "The tradition of the shield maiden is revered among our people, as no doubt it is in yours," she said, holding out her arms beseechingly. "Can you blame us for looking to our own history for succor?"

"The legends of our ancestors are of course inspiring," he said, beginning to wave his arms as though to push the very thought away. "But your clan cannot seriously be planning to put you in harm's way. Why, even now many clans are working to codify laws that would prevent such atrocities from ever occurring."

"Our clan has not participated in these discussions," Geirny said, looking wide-eyed to Aesa for confirmation.

"Perhaps not, but they're very popular ideas, I think. Women's domain inside the threshold, men's beyond, and all that. Simply solidifying what one knows to be right."

"So we can clean up after the damage, but not cause it ourselves?" Aesa scoffed. "Those rules wouldn't protect us. We still see the blood. We still feel the deaths!" she exclaimed, both furious and realizing she'd fallen into a tangential argument. The look on the warrior's face changed from alarm to horror at her outcry, and now he had gone quite stone-faced. Geirny stepped, perhaps unconsciously, between him and his boat.

"Look, if our fathers don't disapprove, it doesn't concern you, now, does it?" she said.

The warrior grew, if possible, even more outraged-looking.

"The safety of his future bride very much concerns Jófreiðr and his family," he said.

"That agreement isn't final, you know," Geirny warned. "In fact, its future is very much in doubt."

"Foolish woman, you would reject a son of the Ylfing?"

"Dear Jófreiðr is the nephew by marriage of the younger son of one of your minor chieftains. I don't think he's really their best offer."

The man's face flushed, and he began to walk with purpose towards his boat. "I shall bring word of your insult back to the clan. Prepare yourselves now, for their judgment will be strong and righteous upon you." Aesa darted after him, searching frantically for words that would smooth all this over. What would her mother do here? What would her *father* do?

She looked around for help, but the other women all stood stock still, mute in their horror. Geirny, more resourceful, clutched at the warrior's arms, but he shook her off impatiently.

"Sir," she begged, making another grab for his arm, "I really think you're taking this a little too . . . whoa!"

Geirny cried out as Aesa brought a smoldering piece of planking firmly into contact with the back of the warrior's head. He turned with a yelp, trying to shove a clinging Geirny off, so Aesa hit him again, and perhaps even again, trying different parts of the skull until her victim collapsed insensate at her feet.

"Well, that's not good," Geirny gasped. "I know!" Aesa shouted. They both looked up towards the skraeling, who took a step backward and raised his hands in the air. "I don't mind," he said, in accented tones. "He's not exactly a friend."

The man glanced warily between Aesa and Geirny, clearly gauging their hostility. Aesa wanted to laugh at the idea that he might consider her a threat, but managed to fight the urge back. She had felled a full-grown man in front of him, after all.

The three faced off uncomfortably over the body of Aesa's victim until Aesa suddenly remembered to check the warrior for breath, and dropped to the ground to do so.

"You're safe with us," Geirny said to the skraeling. "Violence is not usually our first answer."

"Since when?" asked Aesa incredulously, but hushed herself when she saw the thrall's eyes widen further. "I mean, you know how it is," she said apologetically, checking the downed warrior over, and sitting on him as he began to stir.

"Yes," the skraeling said. "I do." He considered them for a moment, a nervous sort of energy sparking between all three. "You know it's in my best interests to help you, right? If I go back without him, they'll kill me. *Anguta*, he'll probably kill me when he wakes up because I witnessed him be felled by a woman. It sounds like you don't really want to kill me, and you could possibly use another set of hands, yes?"

"Yes," Geirny agreed. "Erm, we eat a lot of fish here. I hope you like fish."

"I eat what's fed me," the skraeling said grimly, and Aesa bit her lip and bobbed her shoulders a little at the awkwardness that suddenly flooded her.

With the help of some of the less-anxious bystanders, they managed to bind some dress cording about their now-struggling captive's wrists. Geirny, Aesa, and the skraeling half-carried, half-dragged him up the hill towards the dwellings.

"*Why* do we live in the foothills, again?" Geirny griped, waving airily with her free hand towards the raised eyebrow of a passing acquaintance.

"Drainage," Aesa said shortly, trying to reshoulder her part of the burden. "So our story about how this man got injured is . . ."

"Bonked by a falling piece of half-burnt timber," Geirny said. "Highly unsafe, our *møtehall*, you know. Ought to be torn down. We'll send a message back to Jófreiðr, tell him we're stashing his vassal with our best healer women, and we'll send him back good as new in . . . a while." She chewed the inside of her cheek for a bit. "What happens when we don't send him back?"

"That," Aesa said, "is a problem for another day. Right, new friend—er, what is your name, many pardons?"

"Panuk," the skraeling said, and flashed her a broad smile.

"You don't happen to know how to fight, do you, Panuk?"

"I was a farmer before I was captured. I'll be helpful to you, have no fear, but I'd have to learn."

"Learn, not teach," Aesa said, half to herself, but Geirny still caught it.

"We should learn, shouldn't we?" she replied, mulling over the idea.

Aesa nodded. "I think so. I did more damage than I probably had to, here. Knowing how to disable someone without necessarily murdering them wasn't exactly in our lesson plan," she said, grimacing. "But not just us. Lots of people are going to need to learn, although the old ones may try to stop us, at first."

"You think they wouldn't see the reasons?"

Aesa recalled conflicts with her tall, proud aunts, and shook her head. "I think people categorize threats differently. We're used to war, here. We are not used to women fighting back. I mean, just hearing the idea obviously struck at the very heart of this fine upstanding man, here." She turned her head to query their new companion. "Hey, Panuk, what *is* his name, anyway?"

"Ørlygr. But I call him Putuguq, in my head. Means 'Big Toe' in my language."

"Putuguq, then. Clearly Putuguq felt like I was collapsing our whole future around his head when I suggested we were going to be trained, and we can't trust others not to feel the same way."

"But who can we ask, then?" Geirny asked, stumbling a little under the man's weight. A hand slipped between Putuguq's shoulder and her arm. "Well, definitely ask me, for a start," Nefja said, settling into Geirny's place.

Aesa glanced behind them, and made the startling discovery that the snow had muffled dozens of pairs of feet. Nefja, Dotta, and even Sigrun had apparently been following them for some time. Some though, had a grim sort of cast to their faces.

"Or you could come to your senses. You need to let that man go. You're going to get us killed," one of them hissed, gesturing at the wriggling prisoner. "If you beg his forgiveness and humble yourself properly, the Ylfing might spare us."

Aesa raised an eyebrow at the woman, whose cherubic face Aesa remembered from some of her more abortive handiwork classes. "I don't know if you heard, uh . . ." she began, waving her free hand a bit helplessly.

"Frederikke," the woman drawled. "Thank you for remembering."

"Sorry," Aesa said. "But if you heard our conversation, you'd know that the Ylfing don't plan to spare us. They want to rule us."

"I didn't hear that part," Frederikke said. "I heard a lot about protection and concern and keeping us out of harm's way."

Another woman linked her arm through Frederikke's as she stared defiantly at Aesa. "I heard a lot of unladylike shouting," she added.

"You should have listened harder," said Geirny. "He wasn't going to leave us to govern ourselves."

"Exactly," said Frederikke, now trembling a little in her fury. "He was going to keep us safe."

"We'll keep ourselves safe," Aesa said, unable to restrain her annoyance. "Without the . . ."

"Without our men?" Frederikke broke in. "I don't think so. *We* don't think so. I know you think you're chieftain now, Aesa, but some of us aren't all right with this."

Flummoxed by the accusation, Aesa gasped like a landed fish, and Nefja hurried to her defense. "She yelled at him and then clocked him in the head. He won't forgive us, and you know it. We're just trying to do what needs to be done."

"You well might imagine that you could take the place of a man, Nefja," Frederikke's friend said, raking Nefja's strong form up and down with her eyes, "but some of us don't want to try."

"Well, I do want to try!" a now red-faced Nefja roared. "They took my brother. They took Geirny's mother. They probably took someone from you. If we train ourselves, we might be able to go get them back!"

Frederikke leaned a little away, but her eyes were still flinty. "Think about what you're saying," she said slowly. "You want us to learn to hurt people. We," she indicated a circle with her finger, "don't hurt people."

"No," said Aesa. "You let men do the hurting for you."

"'Rikke, I know you're trying to do the right thing, but so are we," Geirny interjected. "I would let this man go in a heartbeat, if I didn't think we'd be in worse danger because of it."

"It's lovely that you get to decide that for all of us," Frederikke said sweetly.

"We don't have to," Nefja offered. "You like tradition so much? Fight me in single combat, then. Winner's leader, and decides what to do." She leaned towards Frederikke, emphasizing her superior size, and the other woman recoiled again.

"If your ideas were so great, you wouldn't have to use threats and violence to get others to go along with you," another woman protested.

"Gods love a good fight," Nefja said. "Can't see why they wouldn't be on my side. Are we done? Putuguq here's heavy, and he needs a nap."

She hoisted the man's arm back onto her shoulder, turning to head up the hillside. Frederikke clearly wanted to say more, but her friend tugged on her arm, and a cluster of consoling women hurried off, casting dark looks over their shoulders.

But Aesa found that she and Geirny and Nefja were still far from alone in escorting their burden. Many of the women who'd been so hard at work in the clearing that afternoon now walked alongside, their faces a range of trepidation and determination. Members of both free castes, *jarlar* and *karlar*, were in plentiful evidence, with arms even twining around each others' backs as they walked.

Aesa paused for a moment. "So you're all still here . . . because you want to overpower us, or because you want to learn to defend yourselves?"

Sigrun coughed. "I want to learn to defend myself," she said, her jaw set. Aesa looked around at the heads nodding in resolution, and bit back tears. "Well, then," she said, unsteadily. "Let's find ourselves a teacher."

P

IT TOOK SOME TIME to organize a rota to feed and guard their captive, who now slumped in an unlovely cell. Nefja and Geirny conferred with the skraeling Panuk to determine a course of action in case Frederikke and her friends tried to free him.

In that time, Aesa did some calculations and some head counts of the women around her. As her totals increased, hope grew in her heart.

"We have the full complement needed for a warband, and more," Aesa said, voicing the hope out loud as the group hiked out to where the fenced-off farmsteads dotted the landscape. "We could conduct a raid. We don't just have to defend, or sit on our hands until my father comes home. We could get your family back ourselves." Something fluttered in her heart and stomach when she spoke the words. Nefja gasped, and Sigrun arched a speculative eyebrow.

"Are you sure that's, um, a good idea?" Dotta asked. "I mean, it's not that I wouldn't want to try," she added, raising her hands defensively to stave off Nefja's incredulous stare. "It's just—it's all going to be very dangerous, and more than the Skjöldungar will be angry with us for taking up arms, if word gets out."

"If a band of war-women successfully raids the Skjöldungar, I will be very surprised if word gets out at all," Geirny said darkly. "The story, if we even hear it, will likely be unrecognizable."

"A bear attack, they'll claim," Nefja said.

"Dragon," added Sigrun.

"Bondsmen will talk," Dotta said, a little braver now.

"People only believe bondsmen when it's convenient to them," Sigrun said. "And a fighting force of women will likely seem very inconvenient indeed."

Aesa grimaced cheerfully at Dotta. "You're right to be concerned," she said. "To answer your original question, of course I'm not sure it's the best thing. Everyone who goes with me might get killed. My father and his crews may return in a week, and we may all feel very silly and just return back to our fields and our carding combs like nothing happened. But for now, this—this seems right, in the face of everything. I have to do something, and that something could likely involve bloodshed, so I'd better learn how to be good at it."

"You did all right back there," Nefja said, gesturing toward the *ping* meadow with a jerk of her thumb.

"Well, I know enough to swing a club at my opponent's head, but I don't know much about what to do when he swings back at me, except not be where the club lands. Even that's going to take reflex I don't have, which is going to mean practice."

"Can't we try sneaking instead?" Dotta said.

Aesa grinned even more widely. "Of course we're going to sneak. We're going to sneak, and we're going to spy, and we'll use timing and strategy and every resource we possibly have. But if everything goes wrong, I would like to do more before I die than fling my hands in the air. I would like to at least try to keep living."

Dotta grasped her shoulder briefly, and Aesa closed her eyes in gratitude for the comfort.

"It won't be so bad. We've most of us killed already," Nefja said.

"Chickens," someone called from the back.

"Still, life and death—we've held the power in our hands. There just may be more blood, with men. And the gods know we women know how to deal with blood."

There were some chuckles, but a silence fell, wrapping the members of the group in individual contemplation. No one spoke much again until they arrived at the door of Vigi's . . . *Kiaran's* farmstead, Aesa reminded herself. Hearing voices, they trooped around the back to see Kiaran lounging with Ingirun and Mette, a young cloth-cutter's apprentice known mostly for dreamily composing poetry all through lessons. The two women did not look particularly pleased, to Aesa's eye, but Kiaran sprang up with arms extended and began hugging his way through the new arrivals.

"How are you?" he breathlessly asked Aesa when he'd finally made his way back around to her again. "Have you all come to apply to be my wife? It's a big farm, you know, lots of hard work to do." He winked, and some of the younger girls blushed.

"We've come . . ." Aesa stopped, feeling suddenly foolish. Geirny grimaced at her, and she felt a sense of purpose flood through her again. "We've come to ask for your help."

"Well, then, you shall have it!" Kiaran cried, seating himself mock-grandly as though he were a chieftain preparing to hear supplicants. "What can I do for you ladies?"

"We'd like you to teach us to fight," Aesa said. There, she'd said it.

"Ingirun's the one you should apply to, then. Her tongue's the sharpest weapon a woman could wish," he said, smiling to take the sting out of his words. Ingirun shifted where she sat.

"No, I mean—we want you to train us, all of us, in combat. So we can retrieve our people, and protect ourselves until our raid men come home," Aesa said, growing embarrassed again.

"Awww, are you frightened? Dear gentle ones, have no fear. I shall protect you from warbands large and small. Here in my steadinghall, we shall gather, and shut out the howling of the wolves with the sounds of our merry voices. You are welcome any time," he said, flinging his arms out expansively. Nefja snorted, and Kiaran reddened slightly.

"Do you think because I'm here, I'm less fierce and mighty of a combatant than those on raid?" he asked. "Those absent layabouts don't have lands to care for, so they must take their living from others. I," he said, thumping his chest, "know the labor of a real warrior. I wrestle with the land every day—as fierce a fighter as you could ever wish for."

"Good," Geirny said, sweetly. "Then you're perfectly qualified to train us to become real warriors too."

"Teaching requires a master. And before you say it—yes, I'm a master of many things, but I've never taught anyone to fight."

"Just show us what you've been taught," Aesa spoke up. "Unless you're rusty from all that land-wrestling."

"Dare you besmirch the honor of my bright blade?" Kiaran said, chucking her on the chin. "For you of all people should know that our family wields real swords. And though you are all doughty and fierce, your fair arms could not even lift one, I suspect."

Nefja flexed surreptitiously, but this was a problem Aesa had already considered. "Of course you're not going to teach us to use swords," she said. "There's scarcely a handful among us, anyway. We'll use axes. Every household has them, and every one of us wields one near every day."

"And scythes," Nefja pointed out. "We've lots of scythes. And scissors are basically daggers, you know."

"Those are not worthy weapons," Kiaran scoffed.

"But they're what we have," Aesa said, "and surely if we try to train ourselves, we'll engender some needless injury. Can't you at least supervise? Keep us from getting hurt?"

He frowned. "Honestly, I'd rather not. You're right, someone could get hurt, and that's too high a cost for some playacting."

"We're not playacting," said Dotta, outraged. Kiaran and Aesa both blinked at her. "We're scared, it's true, and the best way to not be scared is to do something," she continued, a space clearing around her as people shuffled a little away to give her room. "Teach us what you know. It'll keep us safe, and it'll make you our protector. A hero, even. We'll erect a runestone to your bravery, and we'll be good students. Just teach us." She fell silent, but her face did not lose its burning intensity.

Kiaran looked thoughtful. "I s'pose I could. As long as this stays our secret. No one rats me out to Aesa's father when he returns, yeah?" He looked seriously into each face until they nodded. "Good. Then we'll begin our lessons tomorrow. I'm famished, and there's planting to do." He snapped his fingers decisively, and Aesa let out a breath she didn't realize she'd been holding. The women conferred among themselves, sorting out training regimens and organizing a weapons cache while Kiaran and Ingirun disappeared into the house. Aesa noticed that Mette, Ingirun's erstwhile rival, now hovered near the edges of their group. She smiled. Clever girl, realizing that training with them meant spending time with Kiaran. Or maybe she wished to learn to defend herself too. It felt . . . powerful, she had to admit—knowing that soon she might know how to strike back against those that threatened her. For now, good. That feeling of goodness would probably go away the moment she had to inflict actual hurt on someone else, but—

She shook her shoulders, trying to clear her thoughts. She needed to focus. Mere farm tools, used without concentration, had many times caused injuries, to herself and others she knew. She needed to get her head right, before she picked up a real weapon. And the best place for uncluttering her soul had always been a little hut at the edge of the ocean . . .

She touched Geirny on the arm. "I'm going to visit my Uncle Martyn," she said.

Geirny goggled. "Is he still alive?" she asked, then recovered. "I mean, good. Pass on my regards, and all that. Just make sure you're back tomorrow afternoon, since I get the feeling that great lunk only agreed to teach us to impress you."

"More like he's reclaiming his status from Dotta," Aesa said, but grinned nonetheless.

Uncle Martyn was not her uncle by near-blood, but she had gotten in the habit of calling him that as a small child, since he was the one man around who would tolerate her sticky, grabbing fingers and demands for songs. A distant relative of the sort no one precisely claimed, but no one could quite abandon, since the blood of *jarlar* ran in his veins, he farmed a small plot well past the main village, where he could be conveniently ignored by just about everyone. He and Aesa's father had once been close, but Uncle Martyn had shocked the community by taking a thrall bondswoman as his full and recognized wife, and Aesa's parents had never forgiven him the affront to propriety.

Once she grew old enough to make the trip on her own, Aesa frequently snuck off to visit him and his wife Cynisca, who seemed to regard her with the same tolerant affection one would a large, ill-trained puppy. Uncle Martyn was always puttering about with his boats, trying variations and testing theories out in the small, sheltered inlet near his home, and he put up with Aesa's endless questions with the same patience he'd frequently used while fending off her sticky fingers.

Aesa realized that she was assuming that the raid which had so devastated their village had not made its way down the coast to sack her uncle's tiny farmstead, but the alternative did not bear thinking of, so she shouldered a knapsack and trudged off, hope-filled, to her refuge.

Once, as a child, she had tried to run away to it, insisting that Martyn and Cynisca take her on permanently, but they had only looked at each other sadly, and shaken their heads. Aesa's father had appeared on their doorstep a few days later, flung his protesting daughter over his shoulder, and wordlessly hauled her all the way back to the village. Her mother hadn't spoken to her for a week, furious that Aesa had wasted so much of her father's valuable time. Aesa herself had remained largely uncowed, but concerned that further defiance might bring trouble down on her uncle's head, she kept her visits short and ignorable from then on. With her father and mother absent, she should have had more freedom to go where she willed, but as a prospective bride she discovered that her movements were more circumscribed than ever. Too much time in the company of undesirables, she learned from an earnest wise woman who'd pulled her aside one day, could leave a stain on her character that no self-respecting prospective family would overlook. She'd be the primary instructor of children, after all, and her honor must be beyond reproach.

It was something to consider now, she thought. Would the wise women be curious about the exodus of so many girls to Kiaran's farm every afternoon? Probably, even in the face of their current circumstances. They'd have to come up with a cover story to explain their gatherings, or try to train in secret pairings. *Karlar* women not wealthy enough to support many thralls might soon feel themselves stretched thin in the absence of the helping hands of husbands, brothers, and sons on their farms. Merchant women too would be looking to regenerate their stocks after the depredation of the raid, and frequent absences on workdays would be remarked upon.

Or . . . what would their mothers do about it, if they simply declared themselves to be warriors? After all, those resolved to train made up about a third of the village now. What could the others really do? Aesa pictured the confrontation with her own mother—the contorted faces, the furious, raised voices, the daily fallout—and shuddered. Better to save her energy for learning how to not die. Hopefully.

P

WHEN SHE ARRIVED AT HER UNCLE'S HOUSE, the place looked deserted. Aesa felt her heart jump into her throat. She had to cough before she could voice the passcode. "Are you someone?"

"Everyone's someone at home," came a faint cry from around the back of the building. Aesa clutched her skirts and breathed deeply in relief before hurrying around.

The scene that met her eyes was so pastoral and normal that she nearly burst into tears. Cynisca stood at the end of a half-hoed row in her small plot, waving a greeting. Her uncle sprawled in the shade of their house. He'd evidently been cleaning tools when she arrived. "Hallo, sproutling. I'd stand up, but you know," he said, gesturing at his legs. Broken in a sparring accident long ago, they'd healed poorly, and were now gnarled and twisted. Aesa scoffed dramatically. "Uncle Martyn, everyone knows you haven't a leg to stand on," she said, regaining much of her cheerfulness as she repeated their ancient joke.

"I'll get you something to drink," Cynisca murmured as she passed beyond them into the cool darkness of the house.

"Make it mead-y!" he called to her, before grimacing to Aesa. "She keeps trying to get me to drink this Byzantine swill she bought from a trader."

"That swill, as you call it, is wine like that drunk by the emperors themselves!" Cynisca shouted back.

"That explains why it cost so much!" He turned a beaming face to Aesa again. "So you've come to tell us about your beau, have you? Did his father make a good offer?"

"Um, er, no," Aesa said.

"Wasn't the *ping* just held? Cynisca, the *ping* was just days ago, right?"

"Aesa would know," Cynisca said, handing Aesa a goblet carved with strange animals. At least Aesa thought they were supposed to be animals. The figures had rather more feet than they ought.

"Um, yes, the *ping* was held." Aesa bit her lip, wondering where to start.

"Don't tell me you weren't chosen. You must have been chosen." He peered up into her sorrowful face, and waved abruptly. "Don't worry, we can probably take you on here if we try harder to increase our yields. Or at least supplement your living, until your father comes back. Maybe I can convince someone to buy my work. Cynisca, we must strategize." He put down his flagon, grabbed a pointed stick, and began sketching lines and dots in the dirt.

"We were raided," Aesa blurted out. "They hit the hall at the height of the *møte*, and killed everyone inside."

Martyn's hands stilled, and Cynisca sank to the ground beside her husband.

"Who knows?"

"The Ylfing. I don't think they'll put it about; they're too interested in our own lands for themselves, from what their messenger said."

"They've sent a messenger already?"

"It wasn't originally related. We put them off with reminders that my father and our raids will return any day. I doubt they'll pursue it; they have interests that preclude stirring up trouble." She bunched her skirts between her fingers. "We did, ah, take the messenger captive."

Cynisca's face twisted a little, and Martyn raised an eyebrow.

Aesa said, "We upset him, rather, and things were going to turn ugly." Her face flushed, but Martyn ignored it.

"Upset him how?"

"Well, I wanted to show him that we didn't need to be annexed, because our town isn't undefended, so I told him, we were, ah, learning to fight."

"We who?"

"Um, everyone left."

"So I take it 'everyone left' does not include any actual warriors," he said, leaning back against the side of the house. "And your plan was to arm a bunch of youths and women?"

"Mostly just . . . well, entirely women, in fact." It frightened her to speak the truth so baldly, but it also settled something in her chest, a little, at the same time.

"Maybe I'll have a talk with the messenger, see what can be done there," he said, reaching out for his canes.

"I don't know if that's really an option. I, ah, hit him on the head, you see."

Martyn stopped and twisted around to look at her.

"Several times. Because I didn't know where else to hit him. It's why I need training."

"So you can be even less efficient as a negotiator?" he exclaimed. "You sound possessed by Hermóðr himself, woman!"

"I mean, maybe. I don't feel possessed. I just want to get our people back."

"From the raiders? At least you aim high. Except those who aim too high miss the mark." Martyn sighed heavily and sat back again, closing his eyes.

"I don't think it's such a wild idea. Why do you think we have all those legends if something like this hasn't happened before? Why is it so wrong to arm a woman?"

"Armed women aren't my problem," he said, casting a side-eyed glance at Cynisca, who was not particularly trying to conceal her amusement. "Armed combat is another beast entirely. Your band of feral women may indeed become fiercely skilled, but I don't think one women in a hundred has the necessary temperament for a battlefield."

"They see battlefields all the time," Cynisca said.

"Crucially, not while they're happening," Martyn pointed out. "It's one thing to pick up a man's severed head. It's an entirely different thing to watch it leave his body. We prepare our men for it from the moment they're born, just about. And it's their honor to keep you from having to do the same."

"There isn't a terrible lot of male honor around though, just now, and I don't even think the vast might of yours could save us in case of another raid," Aesa said, trying to make the remark seem light-hearted.

"Ah, but you just told me you don't intend to be defensive. You want to go after the vermin, and make them pay."

"Not make them pay. Get our own back."

"What, precisely, do you think the chance is that you'll get a squad in and out without being spotted, eh? You know perfectly well there will be fighting. And with your unfortunate but inevitable inexperience, there will be deaths that accompany that fighting. If you at least stayed here and dug in, those deaths would serve an understandable purpose, but haring off—bah," Martyn said, waving a hand. "Can you imagine my facing up to your father if I let you go? Not to mention your mother. Ugh, it doesn't bear considering!"

"I'd face up to your mother," Cynisca said to Aesa. "It's the least I could do."

"Woman, don't you encourage her!" Martyn protested while staring, betrayed, at his wife. Cynisca smiled at him, but turned a more serious face to Aesa. "How do you plan to arm yourselves?"

"With handaxes, mostly," Aesa said. "We do have an instructor."

"An instructor?" Martyn echoed, skeptically. "What conscience-less idiot would defy the wrath of the gods and all else that's sensible to instruct you?" He reached for his canes again. "Going to go tell that moron what for."

"Well, I'm not going to tell you who it is if you're just going to beat him over it," Aesa said, affronted.

Martyn goggled at her, sputtering a little. Cynisca spoke again. "Is he a good teacher?"

"I don't know yet. We haven't had our first lesson."

"Well, if he's not, remember that some of us know something about combat, too," Cynisca said, staring meaningfully at Martyn.

Martyn grimaced grotesquely, but his wife did not break her stare. At last he deflated slightly. "I'm not saying I'm all right with this, but I can't exactly spy on you to figure out who your teacher is. It wouldn't be . . . dignified. And this one wouldn't tell me, even if she should," he said, poking Cynisca with his cane. "So fine, come and show us what you're learning every once in a while, so we can make sure you're not going to murder yourself with your own axe."

He sighed disgustedly again and grabbed a curved, polished wooden shape from the pile of his experiments, hugging it as though for comfort.

"Aesa, it's a hard life we lead," he said in a quieter voice. "We lose people every day, nearly. We mourn our losses, because we're mortal, but those we miss are likely laughing at our weak tears from the mead halls of Valhǫll. I know this must seem unfair, my asking you to let the raiders go, but you can make a difference here, as long as you're still alive to do it."

Several emotions jammed up Aesa's heart, all at once, and she had to fight back the tears that welled into her eyes. "I just have a feeling that it's the right thing to do."

"You're going to go wading into danger over a feeling?" he asked, not unkindly. "Must be some feeling."

"I think so," she said. She desperately wished for an echo of that feeling in her chest right now, but she mostly just seemed to be tired. It *had* been there, though, and often, this silvery sort of certainty about what she was trying to do. "Yes, it is," she confessed at last, her face reddening.

"Well, who knows. It might be an instruction from the gods." Her uncle leaned back, folded his hands over his stomach, and closed his eyes.

Aesa blinked at him. "Not to, ah, curdle the moment, but . . ."

Martyn opened his eyes again. "You aren't a good negotiator, are you? First lesson: don't topple your own victories." He sighed. "I just know you should follow impressions from the gods. Frigg told me in a dream it was all right to marry Cynisca, after she proposed, and my life has been immeasurably better ever since." He smiled at his wife, who smiled back sweetly. "The gods know what they're doing."

"Ingirun says the gods don't exist," Aesa said, still testing her boundaries.

"Ingirun, whoever this person is, can say whatever they want. You don't have to believe it. You don't have to believe me, either, come to think of it. But I'll help you if I can," he said. He turned away from her then, reaching over to resume his work.

The conversation clearly at an end, Aesa made her goodbyes, and began the trudge home. A physical fight might be welcome, she reflected, after all these conversational ones. Shivering a little, she sent a prayer winging to Þórr. *Mighty God of War, you may not approve of what we're doing, but please, please help us to not accidentally kill ourselves on our first day.*

CHAPTER SEVEN

AESA SLEPT LATE THE NEXT MORNING. Accordingly, she flung herself into some clothes and snatched up her hand-axe on the way out the door. Sigrun raised an eyebrow at her panting form when she arrived, but said nothing. Geirny, on the other hand, flung an arm across her shoulders. "So glad you're here. We have questions."

"Questions?" Aesa gasped, catching her breath.

"Well, one, for now. Not to insult your taste, darling, but is he always like this?"

"What do you mean?"

Geirny gestured to where Kiaran capered about at the edge of the sports field, lunging and flexing before a small gaggle of early arrivers.

"Ah. No, I think it's 'cause he's got an audience. He's normally a bit more, um, relaxed."

She bit her lip as she watched Kiaran execute a spin that even she knew left his back needlessly exposed, then high-kick an imaginary enemy.

"So this is going to be loads of fun, then."

"Looks like it. He must know what he's doing, though. His mother would have paid for the best."

Kiaran assured them of something similar in a speech not long after, although no mention of his mother was made. He first informed them they had put themselves in the right hands—strong, long-fingered hands, Aesa's brain noted treacherously.

"I don't need to talk about how good I am at what I do," he remarked as he paced on the grass before his seated trainees. "You'll be able to tell. And the more you practice, the more impressed with me you'll be." He winked at Aesa, who then had to squirm to avoid Geirny's gleeful poking.

"I haven't taught women before," Kiaran continued. "But I know something about them." Another wink—but this one was aimed at Ingirun. "Some men think women are soft, weak, gentle creatures," he went on. "Some of you are, but I also know that women are just as capable as men of being feral, vicious, and unthinking traitors to each other."

Aesa tried hard to keep smiling and not even think about glancing in Ingirun's direction.

"You talk of sisterhood as we men talk of brotherhood, but in reality, there is no tie that binds any of us that cannot be severed in a moment's panic. It's important that you know this, because *who here hates running?*"

After a startled moment, several hands went up.

"Learn to love it. Become obsessed with it. For the simple reason that your enemy can't kill what they can't catch. And out there, in the field of battle, if you're slow, your sisters here may not come back for you. Not because they don't love you, now. Not because they don't know that it should be their greatest honor to die by your side. But in the field, your sense of honor may be overwhelmed, for a different sort of instinct takes over. You may retreat, and your sister may discover, to her horror, that she is secretly hoping you'll be slow. Because for each warrior that catches a victim, the faster runner has earned that many more seconds to make her escape."

In the silence that followed, Dotta's cough was explosive. She cleared her throat, and murmured an apology. She shifted a little, then said plaintively, "But how are we to run in our dresses anyway?"

Kiaran's stern mask crumbled, and he flashed her a smile as bright as the sun on snow.

"I have no experience with wearing dresses, so I trust you, who does, to figure it out."

They began practice, unsurprisingly, with running. Although most were good-natured about it, their long dresses did in fact hamper their movement dreadfully, and Aesa discovered as she fell on her face that even kirtling her train over her arm had its hazards. Exasperated, Kiaran moved on to throwing—an activity that Nefja at least seemed to enjoy very much. Weight lifting went less poorly, although Ingirun raised concerns about the general lack of good form. Archery was mostly out, since only a few of them could effectively draw the strings of their families' enormous bows. No one could walk on their hands, although their efforts were again impeded by their dresses, which promptly fell over one's face at each attempt. The idea of wrestling was advanced but quickly dismissed by a blushing Dotta. Aesa wanted to start shieldwork, but the general dismay that met this suggestion led them to finish the day by playing a ball game rather dispiritedly. And everywhere, everywhere, stalked Kiaran—shouting, haranguing, and poking until nearly everyone looked as though they could have cheerfully committed murder.

"I suppose that's one way to prepare us to kill," Geirny said as she flopped on the grass after a particularly exasperating match. Aesa groaned wordlessly at her. Sigrun, lounging nearby, was more philosophical. "My father often said that teachers tend to view students as rocks or seedlings. The way to get the best out of a rock is to grind it until it's polished. The way to get the best out of a seedling is to care for it and tend it until it grows strong. I think Kiaran looks at everyone as a rock."

Aesa overcame her shock at Sigrun's speaking to her enough to nod. "I mean, he was prolly treated like a rock, too. Caring is reserved for invalids and old grannies, with a strong implication that if you need it, you are one." She sighed, looking back at Kiaran's sunlit form. "Still, I suppose it's warranted. It's not exactly like our opponents will try to kill us with kindness."

Geirny pulled up a handful of early weeds and offered them to Sigrun with a flourish. "Do try this seedcake, invader dear. It's simply to die for!"

Sigrun snatched up her own clump of weeds and flung them in Geirny's face. "No, try mine, I insist!" Aesa scrambled away as the fight escalated. "Have more! More!" They ended by rubbing fistfuls of plants and dirt in each other's faces until Geirny opened her mouth too wide in protest and ended up having to spit repeatedly and vigorously to breathe properly again.

The air filled now with giggles and sunshine, Aesa leaned back on her elbows and discovered she felt immensely pleased. People had shown up. Kiaran actually seemed to really be teaching them the way he himself had been instructed, as far as she could tell. They weren't exactly warriors after their first day, obviously, but the sports they'd played were clearly meant to help them develop skills that would be required in combat.

After making the trek to Martyn and Cynisca's steading, however, she learned that her uncle was far less optimistic.

"No offense meant to the honor of this man's mother," Martyn said disgustedly after Aesa recounted their day's activities, "who no doubt paid good coin for his training, but that's exactly the kind of soft landed-gentleman sort of nonsense I'd worried you'd learn."

"It's what I saw young men doing on the township playing fields all my life," Aesa said, feeling more than a little defensive of both Kiaran and her plan.

Martyn shoved aside the mess of sailcloth and cat that had been sitting in his lap. "Yes, but those whelps had something you didn't: lots and lots of time." He reached for his sticks and clumped to his feet. "Cynisca!" he shouted towards the house. "It's as bad as we feared."

Some rustlings were heard from inside the dwelling. The noises stopped abruptly, then through the doorway came Cynisca, bearing two painted and bossed shields. She handed one to Aesa. "There's a set of clubs behind the door. Get them, will you please?"

By the time Aesa returned with the knotty wooden practice clubs, her uncle had perched himself on a tall stump near the door. Cynisca held her hand out for one of the clubs, and with a nod of her head indicated that Aesa should stand across from her. Aesa noticed that an area about four feet square had been cleared of her uncle's usual clutter of tools, material, and prototypes.

"It's a bit small for sparring, isn't it?" Aesa said nervously, and her uncle grunted. "You don't often get a lot of space to yourself on a battlefield. Should be half the size, really, but I think Cyn was excited about getting rid of some of my stuff. Don't think I didn't notice, woman," he said, shaking his stick.

Cynisca merely smiled and said evenly, "Shall we begin?"

"I'm to spar with you?" Aesa asked dubiously, looking over the older woman. She realized that Cynisca's mannish tunic and trousers were eminently more suitable for sports than her own heavy dress, and made a note to dig out some old clothes of her father's. Cynisca tapped her gently on the shoulder with her club. "Yes, so pay attention."

"But . . ." Aesa began to protest, but Cynisca was already looking at Martyn, who said simply, "Commence."

It was the blooming pain in her right arm that made Aesa realize that Cynisca had swung and struck more than anything; Cynisca herself stood calmly, regarding Aesa from a relaxed stance—as unruffled if she'd never moved.

"Ow," Aesa said muzzily.

"Your turn," Martyn called. "Show her what for."

"You want me to hit your wife?" Aesa protested, gesturing with her club.

"I want you to try," Martyn retorted. "Go on."

Aesa made an apologetic face, but her shoulder really did hurt. Cynisca couldn't mind a little revenge, surely. She braced her arm against her shield, adjusted her grip, and swung gently at Cynisca's exposed right side.

Only by the time her club got there, nothing was exposed at all. Aesa watched helplessly as her club hurtled from her hand, having been neatly met by Cynisca's shield.

"Grip's too loose," Cynisca said.

Aesa blinked at her incredulously, then leaned to retrieve her fallen club from the dirt.

"One foot out," Martyn said. "Keep in the square."

"Very helpful, thank you," Aesa grumbled. Her hand stung and her shoulder protested as she squared off again. "I suppose I should defend this time."

"That's the idea," said Cynisca. "Ready?"

"Yep," said Aesa, hoisting her shield. She found herself propelled backwards by the force of Cynisca's blow, and had to scramble to keep from falling out of the square entirely.

"Foot fault," called Martyn.

Aesa glared at him, shook her shoulders, and set her stance. "Ready?" she asked.

"Go," Cynisca replied, and Aesa heaved her club with all her might . . . only to miss entirely and receive a sharp rap across the shins from Cynisca's shield-edge.

"Sorry, sorry," Cynisca said, rising from where she'd ducked, and shaking her head. "Got carried away. That'll count as my strike."

Aesa narrowed her eyes. She centered her body, feeling the connection of the soles of her feet to the ground beneath her. She set her jaw, raised her arm, and struck mightily.

This time Cynisca's answering defense reverberated through Aesa's entire body, and she stumbled backwards all the way into her aunt's gorse hedge.

"Two feet out. You've fled," Martyn called out. "You may never speak at a *ping* again. Oh, wait, you couldn't before. That's all right then." He shrugged while Aesa boggled at him. "What? I don't make the rules."

Aesa turned her exasperated face towards Cynisca again. Her erstwhile partner was crouched down, inspecting her shield for damage. Evidently finding none, she stood up and beamed at Aesa. "Playtime done. Let's do some repetition."

"Where did you learn to fight like that?" Aesa demanded, rotating her sore shoulder. Cynisca's grin widened. "My people taught yours how to fight, darling. And your uncle Martyn taught me some tricks. He's very devious, that one, as he should be. Named for my god of war, you know." The couple smiled at each other fondly until the cat, feeling neglected, leapt into Martyn's lap again.

Cynisca stuck her tongue out at the cat. "To motivate you to study well now, know that tomorrow we'll use sharps."

A sense of foreboding flooded over Aesa. "Sharps?"

"Spears, my girl. Essential!" Martyn cackled.

"Ah," Aesa said, looking nervously at Cynisca's muscled form.

"Better get to learning," Cynisca said with a feral grin.

Later that evening, as the coastal breezes soothed reddened faces and tired limbs, and Martyn puttered about in the kitchen, Aesa regarded Cynisca and realized that something had been nagging at her all day. She shifted on the packed earth that served as her seat.

"Um, Cynisca . . ."

Cynisca's face, sunset-lit, turned to her. "Yes, darling?"

"This may be too personal to ask, but, ah . . . why didn't you kill Uncle Martyn, ah, when you were first captured? I mean no offense to his honor, but you could absolutely have murdered him any time you wanted to, even if you weren't a finely-honed killing instrument, as it turns out."

Cynisca flung her head back and laughed, then leaned back on her elbows and peered at Aesa. "The truth is not very romantic. Or not all of it. Are you sure you want to hear it?

Aesa nodded. "I like truth. Er, well, sometimes I do. I want to hear, though."

Cynisca grinned, then sighed, remembering. "It was not . . . economical to kill him. Food and shelter cost money, and your Uncle Martyn did not have a lot to steal, after he purchased me. I could not lay my hands on enough to take me back across half the world to my homeland, and I would have been hunted, for the first stretch. The work here was not too hard, and he did not try to touch me, so I felt that I could bide my time. And then, after not many days, one morning he threw down his tools, declared thralldom to be terrible, and let me go."

Aesa gasped. "He what?"

Cynisca nodded. "And why am I still here then, you ask? No, not love. Not then, anyway. Eco-nomics. I still had no more money to flee than I had had the day before. So I offered him a deal. I would stay and work the land with him, if he would grant me half of the profits from our harvest. Your uncle knew from experience how much he could grow all on his own, and having a good grasp of the economics himself, he agreed. So we became partners."

"Just like that?"

"Just like that. And then, after some time, I did fall in love, with your uncle, and with this funny land, and with your giant, giant mountains, and I asked him to marry me. And so here I am," she said, rolling her shoulders in an elaborate shrug.

"Do you . . . miss your people very much?" Aesa asked.

"Much much," Cynisca said. "Our plot—it feeds us, but it does not make us rich. So we stay here. It is possible to be free and not free, in many ways," she said, laughing suddenly. "I am not free to leave, and you are not free to, I don't know, fly. But we are both free to do other things that I enjoy, and enjoy," she said, flopping over backwards with both arms outstretched.

Aesa mused for a moment. "And maybe I will learn to fly one day," she said, nodding for emphasis.

"Well, if you do, come back and teach me. Good payment for your fighting lessons," Cynisca said, poking her student with a twig until Aesa cracked into giggles.

CHAPTER EIGHT

THE NEXT DAY, Aesa did not feel very much like laughing. Every muscle protested the thought of getting out of bed, and the fact that she faced not one training session but two that day was enough to make her roll over and turn her face to the wall of her sleeping bench. But the thought of Geirny's disappointment at last propelled her up and into her father's wardrobe, where she dragged out several items that, while enormous, were far more suitable for practice than her own enveloping dresses.

When she arrived at the sports field, she discovered that she had not been the only one to come to this realization. The chests of fathers, brothers, and friends had clearly been raided, and women in various degrees of ill-fittedness regarded each other in some bemusement.

Kiaran was most amused of all. "Going to have to grow you up some before you fill those out properly," he said to Aesa, tugging at her overlong sleeve."

"I need space to put all the mighty muscles I'm going to have," she retorted, grinning up at him. "Um, while I've got you, ah, can we talk about that speech yesterday? 'Learn to run or you'll die,' and all that?"

He smiled and raised an eyebrow at her. "What's your concern?"

"Well, um, my concern is that your speech, if it had gone differently, might have frightened everyone away before we've even started," Aesa said. "You're very ferocious, you know, and we might not have a squad by the time you're done, if it's all like this."

"If they're frightened of the truth, then I want them to leave now," said Kiaran calmly. "I want them to know what they're choosing while it's safe to leave. Panic during your mission would be noisy and costly for everyone. I owe it to you to be realistic about what you face."

"But if too many leave, we can't win. And your speech made *me* want to leave, for a moment."

"Are you going to?" He looked intently into her face.

She caught her breath a little before stammering. "N-no."

He clapped her on the back, cheerful again. "Well, then what have you to worry about?"

"Nothing, I guess," she said, shaking her head ruefully. "What are we going to do today?"

More running turned out to be the answer, as well as more throwing, more lifting, and some log-balancing exercises. Aesa found to her chagrin that too-long trousers contained some of the same dangers as long dresses. In a fit of annoyance, she furiously rolled the legs of her pants until they stuck over her knees, causing Sigrun to gasp in delighted horror and whisper to her friends.

Kiaran wanted them to perform the feat of walking on the oars of a team-rowed boat, but several muddy attempts proved the task too difficult for this group, at least for now. Failure seemed to be the order of the day, in fact, as women, perhaps overtired by the previous day's work, collapsed in droves into the shade at one edge of the clearing. Kiaran stood over them shouting, but most ignored him, some even shoving their fingers into their ears and humming blandly. Mette and Ingirun at last petted him into quiescence; Ingirun pointed out that they had all done their best, and would be better for a break.

Secretly, although the thought rankled, Aesa agreed with Kiaran's frustration. While some of the women were natural athletes, and eclipsed even Kiaran in tests of nimbleness, many others were earnest but incompetent in a way that would have been amusing in other circumstances. As it was, Aesa felt uncomfortable and heartbroken by turns. How much practice would they need before any attempts at rescue wouldn't turn into a bloody rout?

Upon being queried, Martyn was actually more optimistic. "Every lot of young cubs is a bumbly, ungraceful bunch when they first begin," he told Aesa as she and Cynisca helped him assemble his latest miniature ship prototype after their lengthy weapons practice. "You'll see improvement soon enough, if you keep at it. And the ice is still too thick in the channel for the Skjöldungar to be venturing out to any of the good trading ports. They're likely just using our people to help till the farms, in the meantime. Er, have you confirmed that it is the Skjöldungar that have them?"

Aesa shook her head. "We thought it might be too dangerous to send scouts out on their own. We plan to investigate as a group. We're working on a sort of disguise."

Martyn bobbled his hands, considering it. "Well, make sure you're stocking up provisions," he said. "A warband lives and dies by its stomach, you know. And don't forget to set aside livestock for your sacrifices." He puffed up his cheeks and blew thoughtfully. "Have you thought about invoking the souls of our slain at the *møtehall* to aid you?"

"I thought being fire-scorched prevents a spirit from rising to take vengeance," Aesa said. "Isn't that the point?"

Cynisca clicked her tongue before Martyn could answer. "You barely wanted to let her be a warrior; now you want her to become a sorceress too?" she asked her husband.

"I want her to have all the advantages," Martyn said. "It's only smart. Speaking of, I'll make you up some amulets. Find out if any of your company are Týr-cultists, will you? Otherwise I'll just invoke Óðinn on them. You must have someone among your number who can bless them properly."

"Er, yes. Possibly." Aesa said uncomfortably. The natural choice should have been Ingirun, whose healer training would have included invocations of godly blessings. But Ingirun strangely didn't even believe in gods, so how effective would her magic be? Not to mention that Aesa had mostly managed to avoid speaking to Ingirun since the cave, and now she realized the passage of time was likely going to make everything even more awkward.

Seeing the shape of her former friend silhouetted against the sun the next morning brought a rush of bile to her throat, and Aesa found that she could not will her feet to approach, let alone her voice to make a request. She settled for throwing herself into the day's regimen with an explosive determination to get everyone through this without Ingirun's personally needing to invoke the gods' blessings on her uncle's amulets. And the grueling work helped. In fact, she lost herself in it that day, and the day after, and the day after that.

Some days later, the routine of train-hike-train-sleep erupted in spectacular fashion. Aesa found herself being boisterously roused from her bed by an excited Geirny.

"It's still night time," Aesa protested, grabbing weakly as her friend peeled the coverlets away from her still-chilly body.

"It's barely night time," Geirny replied heartlessly. "You need to get up. Your man's throwing us a feast." She picked up a discarded overdress from the floor, wrinkled her nose at it, and dove into Aesa's clothing chest for a fresher one.

"Those words you just said don't make any sense," Aesa complained.

"That's because someone wasn't paying attention today, clearly," Geirny said, shoving Aesa's arms through the straps of the overdress. "Kiaran invited us all to his house this morning, and I thought you weren't really listening, but you hared off to wherever before I had a chance to ask you." She ruthlessly strapped shoes to Aesa's feet, then frowned and set about trying to restore sleep-mussed hair to order. "If I was in love, I'd pay attention when my love talks."

"I tend to zone out a little when Ingirun and Mette fawn over him," Aesa admitted. "It keeps me from trying to murder them when we're sparring partners. And they were in such ridiculous form today! Also I'm not in love."

Geirny quirked an eyebrow. "Right. You're not in love, which is why you try so hard not to be the best at everything so he won't praise you." She snatched up a handful of ornaments from a nearby table and strategically affixed them to her friend's person. "Except for how you moon at him all the time. And how you literally want to kill your rivals. Pssh, woman, you're just hedging your bets in case you lose out. Now come on!"

She tugged at Aesa's arm, Aesa snatched up her weaponry, and they burst from the dimness of the house into a night brilliant with stars. "If I miss out on all the *reinsdyrstek* because I came to check on you, I will be very annoyed."

CHAPTER NINE

KIARAN HAD ENACTED A REMARKABLE TRANSFORMATION on part of his land—turning a fallow field into a feasting ground apparently overnight. A sumptuously-draped raised platform stretched over what had been a rough field, and a constellation of torches flared at every corner. Plank tables groaned under the weight of trenchers piled high with fragrant food. From her seat, Dotta hoisted a flagon to Aesa. Kiaran looked in the direction of the salute and came quickly over. Aesa glimpsed Ingirun rolling her eyes before Kiaran's bear hug blotted out the sight.

"Where have you been?" he demanded. "I tried to save you some pastry, but Sigrun may have eaten all of it."

"I don't believe it," Aesa said firmly. "Sigrun doesn't eat."

"She should. She'll grow too thin, and everyone will think her mother keeps a bad table. No one wants to marry into an ungenerous family." He winked at her. "Let's get you and Geirny here a place, shall we?"

After some good-natured shoving, Aesa found herself wedged on a bench in between Geirny and a girl whose name she could never quite recall. Geirny scanned the table.

"I don't see any *reinsdyrstek*, but I'll try to be nice and pretend it wasn't served at all," she said, poking a plate of salted fish with her knife before spearing some bacon.

"I meant to ask on our run down here: why is Kiaran doing all this, anyway?" Aesa asked.

"Didn't say," Geirny replied around a mouthful. "But who am I to argue with food that I didn't have to cook?"

"I think you're about to find out," said the girl on Aesa's left. She gestured with her knife towards where Kiaran was climbing onto a space in the center of the long bench across from them. He cleared his throat and flung his arms out wide, waiting for conversation to still.

"Welcome, my friends!" he called out. "I regret that my hall is not large enough at present to correctly host our mighty army, but I shall begin construction to expand it so we may celebrate as we shall no doubt deserve in the future." He waited, and seemed gratified by an answering wave of applause.

"My dear pupils, you have become the pride of my heart; as great an army as a chieftain could ever hope to raise." There was much table-pounding and whistling at this. He paused again for quiet before he continued. "Accordingly, I hope you have behaved like true warriors and brought your weapons with you, because tonight I plan to lead you out after those who so brutally destroyed our peace."

He did not need to wait for silence this time; it fell like a heavy blanket over the rows of upturned faces. "Eat well, my lovely soldiers, and be of good heart. We cannot but prevail!"

He signaled to his left, and a couple of bondsman musicians struck up a tune, covering the sibilance of dozens of nervous whispers. Kiaran climbed down from his perch as Aesa extracted herself from the bench, making murmured apologies to her seatmates for her clumsiness. She fixed what she hoped was a reassuring smile to her face as she hurried down the row. "Might I have a word?" she hissed in Kiaran's ear.

A flicker of irritation crossed his face, but he smiled and bowed to Ingirun and Mette before joining her a little way from the table. She hooked her arm under his to pull him out of earshot.

"Kiaran, I know you've worked awfully hard to knock us into shape. And I trust your judgment, I really do. But don't you think this is all a little, uh, hasty?"

He smiled wryly at her. "Not eager to face your first battle? I understand completely. Don't worry, I'll make sure you're safely behind me when we set out."

"Ah, no, it's more like I don't think we're ready to go at all. Any of us. We barely know what we're doing, and . . ."

Again came the sympathetic smile. "I know it's frightening to you, but the weather's starting to get better. The Skjöldungar won't want to feed our people for longer than they have to, if they're not planning to keep them. They may be looking to sell, and we've got to get there before that."

"My Uncle Martyn says it's still too early for them to be on the move."

Kiaran wrinkled his brow. "Your Uncle Martyn? Is he still alive? I should pay him a visit." His face smoothed, and he looked at her seriously. "But while you know I respect your uncle with all my heart, you can't say he's exactly the most tactically-minded fellow ever. Besides, shouldn't we at least go and confirm we've got the right raiders before we plunge into the depths of the Skjöldungar stronghold?"

"Have they got a stronghold? I didn't realize they'd fortified."

"That's my point. You don't know, and neither do I. We need to do some intelligence gathering, and we need to do it right away."

"Kiaran, we can't move yet. Soon, yes, but not yet. Most of these women just picked up a weapon for the first time a handful of days ago."

"Funny, I recall a little bird telling me you've been wielding hand-axes your whole lives."

"Not to kill with!"

"Sometimes to kill with."

"Livestock! Look, maybe a smaller group could go. You, me . . ."

"Trying to get me alone, are you?"

"Gah!"

She rolled her eyes at him and flung her hands in the air, but he simply regarded her, smiling thoughtfully. "Aesa . . . come with me for a little bit." He glanced towards the edge of the forest, then looped a finger under her elbow and tugged gently. Aesa looked into his eyes, twisted her mouth, and then allowed herself to be led over the damp ground, albeit grumpily.

"We can't leave them too long. They'll get drunk."

"They're grown women. They can take care of themselves."

"Yes, but they're scared now. You scared them. Come on, now, Kiaran, what do you mean by launching us so early?"

"I know what I'm doing."

"Maybe you do, but we don't yet. And a lot of good we'll be to you tonight after you've gotten us sauced up." Aesa rolled her eyes back towards the feast table, and flinched when Kiaran laid his finger on her lips.

"Quietly, my dove. I've brought you over here to share my secrets, and I need you to take it down a notch."

"What secrets?" Aesa asked, resisting an urge to snarl.

He smiled infuriatingly at her, but refused to answer as they walked further into the shadowy, crackling embrace of the faintly moonlit woods. Aesa willed her eyes to adjust before she smacked into a tree branch. At last Kiaran glanced over his shoulder and, apparently satisfied, stopped. "What if I told you . . . you won't need to fight tomorrow?"

"Me? Or any of us?" Hope rose in her chest. "What have you got planned?"

"Now look, this has to be absolutely between us, you understand?"

"Yes, Kiaran, of course, but what did you do? Who did you get?"

He grinned. "Let's just say that tonight, these women are going to strap on the little armor they have, shoulder their sad, pitiful weapons, and we're going to creep around the woods until everyone's gotten really, *really* scared, and they'll be completely and forever grateful to me if we just head home."

Aesa stared at him. "So . . . you're running a training exercise?" She started to smile. "No, this is really good. It won't seem so bad when we go to do the real thing. Clever man!"

He caught her shoulder. "Aesa, it will be the real thing."

"What? So we're like a decoy?" She pushed on his chest. "Stop playing with me. Did you get mercenaries, then? That's wonderful! Why are you being so weird about it?"

He compressed his lips for a moment. "Look, I'm only telling you this because I need you not to hate me." He took a deep breath. "You need to understand, we're not going on a real raid. At all. Ever." He grabbed her shoulder again before she could dart away from him. "Aesa, nobody really wants to go. They're scared, and they don't want to let you down, and no one can bring themselves to speak up. I get it. It would seem like betraying their families. I'm not going to lead them into battle feeling that way, though."

"You don't know they feel like that. Did you actually ask?"

"If I asked, they would just lie, to save honor. But I don't have to ask. You said it yourself—they're so scared. Just look at them!"

"They're scared because they don't know what they're doing. We've barely discussed plans. We've barely practiced at all. But we're trying because of our families. And you were going to just . . . do you have any concept of what this means to us?"

"They're my family too! Do you know how many friends I had in that group? Boys who looked up to me? Young women who . . ." He choked, coughed, and looked away.

Aesa grabbed his arm. "Exactly. That's why we've got to get them back. How can we just give up like this? You know what could be happening to them!"

He wheeled on her, startling her into letting go. "Or maybe it's already happened, have you thought of that? Maybe you'll get there, and you won't find anyone. If someone gets captured, or killed trying to get there, it'll be one more thing that didn't have to happen. Yes, the raid that day was terrible. Devastating. I miss everyone so much. But it's a normal part of life, to die, and we owe something to them. To be alive, now. To not kill ourselves trying to save them, when they may already be sold or dead."

They stared at each other. Aesa discovered she was shaking. *Go,* the voice inside her said, quietly, and the fear ebbed a little bit.

"I'm going. I have to. I can't live like this. They need to be rescued. I'm going."

"Aesa . . . no, you're not."

"I am."

"You're not."

"Kiaran, you don't have a say."

"I do."

"Why?" She stared at him, willing him to finally admit it.

"Because I'm still bigger . . . and stronger than you." He moved towards her, then, and she read his intentions on his tear-streaked face.

"Oh, no, you're not. *Oh, no, you're not!*" Aesa screamed, wrenching her shoulders as he tried to pin her elbows behind her back.

Everything she'd learned from him drained out of her head at the shock of feeling his hands on her. She struggled frantically as she tried to recall something, anything she could use. Cynisca's stern face floated to her mind's eye. What were her unarmed combat essentials? Yelling, check. But then what?

Her panicked mind focused for a moment, and Aesa stomped on Kiaran's instep and flung all her weight forward towards the ground. The combination of pain and surprise broke his hold, and she rolled forward and back onto her feet.

Aesa sprang up, spared one glance over her shoulder to confirm his position as he charged after her, and bolted for the forest edge, screaming as she went.

The relief of hearing voices call back in response lent fire to her legs, and she hurtled up the path. "Geirny! Dotta! Nefja! Sigrun! To *arms!*" she called, and burst out of the tree cover into the firelight at edge of the clearing.

Her friends had risen to their feet around the table. They were clearly confused, but nevertheless determined to show willing, and clutched weapons in their hands. Aesa bolted around the table to put it between her and Kiaran and hid behind Nefja's back, resting her face briefly against the taller woman's shoulder blades.

The group straightened when they heard more crashing in the underbrush. "What is that?" Sigrun hissed.

"Kiaran," Aesa gasped. "He's trying to stop us from going."

"Is that true, Kiaran? Are you trying to stop us?" Geirny asked loudly. Aesa looked up to see Kiaran stumble out of the woods.

"From going to your deaths? Yes," he panted, leaning forward to rest his hands on his knees.

"Don't act noble, Kiaran," Aesa spat. "You dishonor yourself by your betrayal of us."

"Being smart isn't dishonorable. And this whole venture—you all have to know, deep down, this isn't smart." He calmly rose to his full height and gestured beseechingly to the pale, uncertain faces before him.

Aesa stepped forward, instinctively trying to block him from the others' sight. "We've worked so hard for this. This plan is all we have. You said it yourself, our family might be sold soon."

"Yes. And we will mourn them. But Aesa, that's life. You know as well as I do. That's why we must live so fiercely, every day. Besides, your father and mother will come back, and they'll exact your vengeance for you. I want you—I want everyone here to *be here* for them to come back to."

"Well. Thank you for your concern," Geirny said. "Anything else you'd like to add, before we take our leave?"

"No," cried a voice, and Mette climbed over the bench so she could better address the group. "We can't leave. He's our leader." She looked defiantly at Geirny. "We owe him our allegiance, and anyway he's the one who knows what he's doing." There was a murmur of some agreement, to which Geirny raised an eyebrow.

"What? No, he's not our leader," Aesa exclaimed hotly. "Anyway, he's lost his honor by lying to us. He's not fit to lead us."

"Lost my honor, you say? Over a trick that could save lives? That's quite the claim, Aesa," Kiaran said, his brow slightly furrowed. "I let your slander go the first time, but to deliberately repeat it—that's a mortal insult, some might say."

"It's not an insult if it's true." She lifted her chin.

"If it's true. That's the question, isn't it. How to prove that, though? Have I lost honor by trying to keep you alive?" He paused, contemplative, then snapped his fingers.

"Friends, we are a people of many traditions, are we not? One of the most important, the most dear to us, is that the leader of a warband must be its fiercest warrior. The strongest. The best."

Kiaran looked earnestly into each face, one by one. "The gods demand so little of us, but this one thing, though, they do ask—that we send our best and most honorable to lead. And they have granted us a way to make that determination, without fail."

He turned to Aesa, his eyes glittering in the torchlight. His face was grim.

"Aesa, daughter of Ottar, I am Kiaran, son of Vigi. I challenge you for leadership of this warband. I challenge you to holy combat."

CHAPTER TEN

AESA FOUGHT TO STAY PRESENT while factions around her discussed the terms of the duel. Kiaran had left almost immediately after issuing his challenge—possibly to retrieve shields so they could make her acceptance nice and official. Trial by combat was quickly dismissed—"He doesn't want to *kill* her!"—but the lack of expendable equipment made a shield-splitting trial problematic. At last they settled on a modified sort of holm-going, in which each combatant would be allowed one shield and two rest periods. Since their stretch of coastline lacked the traditional small island—the holm part of the holm-going—women started to move benches and torches to mark out the appropriate fighting field. Ingirun began the required consecration rituals, her face shadowed and unreadable.

It was the sight of Kiaran returning that brought Aesa back to herself. It was time for strategy. Problem one, evidently—trying to convince her body that he was, for now, an enemy. She must convert her instincts into the desire to hurt. Even thinking about it made her wince, and Geirny peered anxiously at her face.

"Does she look pale?" Geirny asked Dotta. "I can't tell."

Dotta stood on tiptoe to look, and wrinkled her brow.

"I'm fine," Aesa said, her teeth gritted against the bile that was beginning to churn in her stomach. "I just need to . . . breathe more." That was it. Breathe, and then think. She filled her lungs, forcing her chest to open, and blew the air out slowly. The sense of light-headedness began to fade, as well as the feeling of crawling bugs in her belly.

A summoned thrall ran to Kiaran's side, holding two cylinders of wood. Another handed him a helm, while a third stood poised to step forward, holding a shield. Both good news and bad, then, since while the training batons lacked edges, they weighed about twice as much as her regular axe. She bounced on the balls of her feet, still working the air through her lungs. As Kiaran lowered the long nose-guard of the helm over his face, something in her heart shifted too. The mask would make this easier. She signalled for her own helm, and Geirny helped seat it correctly, while Dotta threaded the shield onto Aesa's arm. She focused on her breath, willing control over her spirit. Something nagged at the back of her mind.

"If we're not using edged weapons," she said to her helpers, "then how are we counting the win?"

"First with both feet off the hide loses," said Geirny. "Would you rather it was most wounded?"

"No," said Aesa hurriedly. "It's just . . ." *It's just that Kiaran's nearly a head taller than I am, and with one good shove he could probably send me tumbling right out of the ring.* But did she really want to use an axe against him? Of its own accord, her brain began to imagine the sight of her axe blade chopping into the skin of his arm, and she forcibly redirected her thoughts to her breathing with a quickness.

Preparations were rapidly finished, and the next thing she knew, she was standing across from Kiaran in an empty space, surrounded by spectators. His face was stern under the helm, and she looked away, focusing on the mood of crowd instead. Some women were clearly anxious for her, but not all. Mette's eyes glittered with anticipation. Aesa looked to Ingirun, but she'd disappeared behind the crowd, no doubt preparing her salves and remedies for bruised flesh.

Kiaran seemed energized by all the attention, and this time grinned broadly at her when he saw her looking back at him. In the torchlight, the smile did not look entirely friendly. Still, she didn't need friends in this space. She was, in fact, surprised to discover a sort of sense of being at home in this marked square, with its by-now-familiar stretched hides and ritual poles and pegs.

Problem two was now evident, though—with the arena limited to nine feet on a side, she'd barely have room for the kind of dodging Cynisca had instructed her to use against a larger opponent. Problem three was once again her clothing: the long skirts Geirny had picked out for her in haste for their dinner would likely hamper any kicks she might try, and anyway Kiaran's long reach combined with his weapon would probably put him safely out of strike range of her foot. So what was her battle plan? Her thoughts tumbled over each other as she sought and discarded options.

Kiaran slapped his baton against his shield, breaking her reverie. "I've issued you a formal challenge, Aesa. Are you going to accept it?"

She lifted her chin and looked him squarely in the face, taking the opportunity to note the way the helm fitted his head, the way he hefted his shield, and the stance of his unarmored body.

"Yes," she said clearly and firmly, and a buzz of excitement rippled through the crowd in response. She approached and tapped the boss of his shield with her baton; the ritual sign of acceptance and readiness having been made, Kiaran settled back into his right foot and prepared for their bout to begin.

He therefore had his weight in the wrong place to recover when Aesa immediately launched herself through his too-casual guard, clubbing the side of his neck at a firm and deliberate angle with her baton and driving her shield into his side. She used her pivot to drive her knee into his stomach, and although her skirts did in fact seem to blunt the blow, he was still off-balance and gasping when she slammed her foot into his gut. He dropped his baton to grab reflexively at her leg, and the imbalance from the resulting struggle brought them both flailing to the ground.

The crowd rippled away from the boundary markers to give them space. Kiaran's head and shoulders were now technically outside the line, but he seized Aesa's ankle and shoved, using the momentum to help himself roll forward until he knelt on the hem of her dress, effectively trapping one leg. As she frantically tried to free the fabric, he brought the edge of his shield briskly down on her arm repeatedly until she relinquished her hold on her weapon.

"End it, Aesa," he said, nearly spitting into her face. "Let me stop before I do real damage."

She didn't waste her breath in a reply, instead seizing the edges of sleeves brought close by his clutching hands. She wedged her left foot against his right bicep and dragged his left arm across her body, banging her shoulder painfully on his shield. Crying out at the shock, she nevertheless braced her other foot against his knee for a moment, then struck sharply, knocking his leg out from under him.

Aesa rolled until she had nearly braced herself over him, but he found leverage and heaved until she found herself flying sideways. She snatched up her club and flung herself on his back, wrapping her legs around his body and pushing, *pushing* the baton into his throat while his hands scrabbled at her arms, scratching and trying to find purchase. Here her voluminous sleeves were at last her ally, for he wasted valuable time trying to yank and tug the fabric as slowly, implacably, she pressed the breath out of him, trying all the while not to cry.

His grip slackened, but she held the choke, suspecting a trick, before at last determining his unconsciousness to be unfeigned, and lowering him to the ground.

"Feet!" hissed Nefja into the hushed stillness, and Aesa grimaced at the necessity.

Near sobbing, she extracted herself and her skirts from under Kiaran's prone form, then quickly and carefully as she could, heaved and levered his body until at last both feet lay clearly outside the arena boundary. No one moved until moments later, Kiaran began to flinch and stir. Dotta quickly untied her sash and knotted it firmly about his wrists and hands.

"Is that necessary?" Mette protested, and Dotta looked at her sharply.

"Do you really think it isn't?" she asked, quirking an eyebrow.

Mette blushed and glowered, but settled for helping Dotta lift the bound Kiaran to a seated position, as Ingirun descended in a whirl of skirts to bathe his brow.

"So, um, I guess we'll need to find you someone else to marry," Geirny muttered to Aesa under her breath as they stood watching. Aesa winced.

Nefja, attaching a different importance to the moment, broke forth in a full-throated cry.

"Behold our leader through rightful combat!"

The watching group shivered a little, but enough answering cheers met Nefja's own that Geirny nudged Aesa in the back until the erstwhile combatant stepped forward, carefully not looking at her still mostly-prone opponent. She did not feel triumphant. She felt sicker than she'd ever felt.

"I will try to lead you as you would wish to be led," Aesa at last said haltingly, "and bring honor to my father's name. We will reconvene at the practice field in two days time, to continue preparing to reclaim our loved ones."

There was a small smattering of applause, but most of her new army seemed drunk and a little dispirited after all the excitement, and Aesa was glad to let them trickle away one by one into the night. She at last brought herself to look at Kiaran, who was being gingerly patted by Mette. They both were clearly making a point of not looking at her.

"Do we need a guard on him, do you think?" Aesa quietly asked Dotta, who, with Geirny and Nefja, had stayed to help Ingirun clear up the ritual objects. She was not quiet enough, though, and Mette's lip curled in response.

"No, we don't need a guard on our friend," she hissed at Aesa as she bathed Kiaran's brow. "Ingirun and I will see to his recovery, and make sure his bondsmen don't get any ideas." She looked darkly towards a thrall extinguishing torches, and the woman bobbed a sort of anxious curtsey and hurried away.

Aesa was swaying on her feet, but stared after the woman. According to the rules of holm-going, some of Kiaran's property might now be hers? Her pounding head meant she couldn't recall all the formalities right now. But seeing the thrall woman cringe away from Mette had set Aesa's blood boiling. She imagined Cynisca in that woman's place, and the idea made her dizzy.

Aesa approached Geirny, glad that she had only stumbled a little on the way. "Don't I have rights here now?" she said, gesturing at the farm. "Aren't I owed something from Kiaran?"

Geirny put down the bag she was holding. "What do you mean?" she asked, her face wary.

"Some of Kiaran's people. I could claim them and let . . ."

Geirny, after a frantic glance at Mette, threw an arm over Aesa's shoulders and pulled her off to the side. "Whatever you were going to say, don't. Kiaran's already going to be angry, but his honor and the witnesses should keep him in check. Claiming his people would make him *killing* angry, though, for more reasons than one. We've enough problems on our hands without him being sure he'll starve this fall because he's got no one to plant in spring. One thing at a time."

Aesa bit her lip. Kiaran's anger was a fearsome thing. She also knew from time spent on the farm that many of Kiaran's bondsmen had their own strong sense of pride, and might not thank her for charging in and mucking about in their problems without consulting them first. She thought about asking Cynisca how best to approach them. Honestly, the whole thing made her feel quite nauseated. In fact . . .

Nefja looked up at the sound of retching from a nearby bush, and smiled wryly. "Our fearless leader?" she asked Dotta, who had also paused in her work.

"Not so fearless, I think," Dotta said. "Which I suppose is a good thing, as long as she doesn't freeze up."

Nefja nodded. "We'll see how she does with training."

Dotta put down her basket and headed for the now-noisome bushes, quietly echoing Nefja's words to herself. "We'll see."

ΦΓ

By the time a cheerful, unflinching spring sun had dawned the next day, all Aesa knew for certain was that she wanted to murder every bird within a mile radius. Geirny discovered early that morning that she was not a natural nurse, but upon being informed that fetching Ingirun was right out, had good-naturedly learned the passwords for approaching Martyn's house and now returned with a smiling Cynisca in tow.

"Has my little lamb hurt herself in a great dreadful battle?" Cynisca cooed in a syrupy voice as she stepped over the threshold. Geirny giggled appreciatively and excused herself to run off to her daily tasks, leaving Aesa to stare at Cynisca aggrievedly.

"I love you and I cannot begin to say how much I appreciate your coming, but what do you mean by speaking to me in that filthy way?" Aesa said, burying her face back in her coverlet once she felt a sufficient impression had been made.

Cynisca grinned. "Can't have your friend blabbing about my dour and surly self to her wealthy friends," she said, setting down her basket. "Martyn and I are safe because we're entirely not-scary to others. Speaking of scary, let's see the rest of those bruises, eh?" She prodded Aesa until the latter produced the injured arm. "Oooh, this is a beauty, is it not?"

Aesa groaned at her, and then whimpered with sincerity as Cynisca's exploration hit a particularly sore spot. Cynisca stuck her tongue out. "What do you have to be so grumpy about? You won the fight, didn't you?"

"Yes, but my innards still feel like goop, and I turned my stomach inside out afterwards," Aesa said. "What kind of warrior does that?"

"A normal one," said Cynisca firmly. "You think your father isn't frightened before a fight? What kind of person doesn't get scared before they go into battle?"

"Berserkers don't," Aesa said, and hissed as Cynisca tied an herbal poultice of some sort to her arm with wide strips of fabric.

"Berserkers aren't real," Cynisca said, "and if they were they'd be a menace, not a model. Being a real warrior means not just being ready to strike, but being clear-headed about the opponent's striking back. Now hold still." She tied the ends of the bandage in a tidy knot, then stood up and began rummaging through Aesa's food stores. Aesa caught a worried expression crossing her face.

"What?"

"Eh, your father is just cutting things a little closer than I'd like." Cynisca pulled a hunk of salt meat out of a cupboard and sniffed it. "He left you money, yes? Give me some, and I'll square you up when I go marketing."

Aesa closed her eyes against an incipient headache. "What's left of my money is on the shelf below that. He assumed I'd have my bride price to live off by now. Is the sea channel clear enough for marketing, then?"

"Just the edges, like your uncle says. Not enough for big boats.

You don't need to worry yet about our people." The sound of knife on wood heralded Cynisca's progress on food, and Aesa's stomach rumbled despite itself.

"Father probably can't get back because of the ice," she mused.

"Mm," Cynisca murmured in agreement, and continued her chopping. The percussive rhythm was loud, but oddly soothing in its homey-ness.

"Cynisca?"

"Yes, darling?"

"Is all of this a terrible idea?"

The chopping stopped. Aesa opened her eyes to see that Cynisca had closed her own. She reopened them after a brief moment, and smiled. "We may decide so later. But for now, who is to say?" She shrugged and gathered the mess of dried herbs and meat into a bowl, then wrinkled her nose at it.

"You don't think I should, I dunno, convince everyone to stay here and wait for my father?"

Cynisca rolled her eyes at Aesa before turning to look through the food stores again. "Didn't you have a great big walloping fight over that yesterday?"

"Yes, but I've had time to think about it, now." Aesa squeezed her eyes shut against the sunlight, and felt tears leak out onto her cheeks. "Maybe Kiaran was right," she said miserably. There was a silence, then Aesa heard the rustle of cloth as Cynisca made room on the sleeping bench.

"I'm not a wise woman," she said at last. "I don't tell you to go, or not go. I don't know what is right, because I can't see the future. What I do know is this: we are never actually safe where we are. Always are enemies, or sickness, or even just change right around the corner. Always danger. Even here at home, in bed, with the sun shining and the birds yelling right outside your window." She made a face. "The fact is, I could slip on some ice right outside your door and break my leg and become ill and die, all because I made the mistake of getting up today."

"Right," said Aesa, pulling the coverlet over her face. "I'll just stay here then and not move." Cynisca chuckled, patted the furs near Aesa's face, and spoke again.

"But I remember a fierce young woman telling my husband that she had a feeling—a feeling so strong—that she was doing the right thing. And she was willing to stand up to her uncle, and aunt, and her father, and mother, and the whole village, and do it anyway. Do you remember that?"

There was a pause. Cynisca seemed to actually want an answer. Aesa folded the coverlet back down. "Yes," she said reluctantly, not meeting Cynisca's eyes.

"Do you feel that way now?"

"I feel hungry," Aesa said. "Bleh. Feed me."

"So, all right, you don't feel that feeling right now. Here is the question, then: are you going to act on it anyway?"

Aesa at last met Cynisca's calm gaze, but her vision felt blurred. Her mind's eye filled with an image of Kiaran, helmed and terrible against a backdrop of night sky and torchlight. The image shifted to one of Kiaran unconscious and helpless. That picture was replaced by one of another hapless youth: Sveni. She'd never gotten his shield back to him. She pictured Geirny's mother, and Gnupa the butcher, and a plume of fire fading to grim smoke in a burning valley. She remembered the chill of the cave seeping into her bones as she'd crouched in silence, waiting for the marauders to leave.

Yes. "Yes," she said again, uncertain if she'd spoken aloud the first time. "Yes, I want to do it. But Cynisca—Kiaran won't help us anymore. We'll need you to finish our training."

It was the older woman's turn to flinch. "No," she said, softly. "You, is one thing." She shook her head. "Everyone else . . . that way leads to no good."

"I thought you couldn't see the future," Aesa teased, but regretted it when Cynisca raised her eyes back to Aesa's.

"Some things are obvious," Cynisca said, hissing a little on the last sibilance. "A thrall who can kill? That looks like danger to everyone who is not a thrall."

"Former thrall," Aesa said.

Cynisca hunched her shoulders. "Not a comforting difference, to most," she said, setting the dish down. "You'll do fine. Teach what I taught you. Tell them you learned from your father. Don't forget to eat that," she said, pointing to the bowl.

The room dimmed briefly as Cynisca stepped through the doorway and was gone. Aesa tried to push herself off the sleeping bench to follow, but instead fell back in a heap as her entire body protested vociferously. She glanced at the bowl, but her stomach threatened to join her body's rebellion.

Aesa closed her eyes. Fine. It was time to plan, anyway. She sighed, lay back, and tried to think leader-like thoughts.

Instead, she dreamed. It was only after she'd leapt out of bed to get away from the insects crawling on her covers that she realized she had actually been asleep. She resisted the urge to brush the coverlet down, half afraid that her hand would actually encounter the strange, spindly bodies of the bugs her subconscious mind had conjured up. Also, her dream self had been pretty sure the insects were poisonous.

She looked around the moonlight-painted room, trying to decide if she should risk sleep again or not. The space felt alien somehow—

unwelcome and terribly cold. Aesa made a face, then flung open the cupboard which contained her father's woodworking tools.

The results of her insomniac spate of work caused some exclamation the next day when the army-in-training arrived at the playing field to see it dotted with half-human forms on stakes.

"Um," said Geirny upon arrival. Sigrun actually recoiled when she glimpsed them through the early morning mists. It was Dotta who, ever pragmatic, simply walked forward and prodded one of the ropy straw-and-wood figures with her axe.

"Oh, for practice," she said.

"Exactly," said Aesa. "I've noticed we don't really swing at full speed right now. We're too concerned with hurting the other person."

"I wish they had heads," said Nefja. "I want to try lopping one off."

Sigrun glanced sideways at her, but Aesa merely shook her head.

"We're not going to use axes, unless you want to volunteer to make repairs after. Anyway, we've got conditioning practice to do first."

Nefja stuck her tongue out at Aesa, who promptly flung her hands on her hips and stuck out her own tongue. The standoff might have continued indefinitely if Geirny hadn't sighed and poked them both in the stomach.

"I'll lead the run," she said, and whistled sharply to get everyone's attention. "Fall out," she called, taking off, and behind her a scraggly line of women formed up and began to make its way around the playing field.

"Something like a real army," Nefja said as she watched them.

"Something like," Aesa said, "but not enough. We ought to start thinking about who should come on the rescue mission and who should stay as rear guard."

"It'd be a terrible insult to the honor of anyone asked to stay behind," Nefja said carefully.

Aesa grimaced. "Am I going to have to pick my squad by dueling everyone here?"

"Perhaps," Nefja grinned. "But we both know I'd win in a fight between us, so there's at least one you can skip. I'll be going along to personally rescue my brother, thank you very much."

Aesa had actually forgotten about Magnus, Nefja's large but shy brother, and grimaced again before darting down the slope to organize weapon checks.

The morning wore on, and Aesa, despite some hiccups, was fairly happy with her performance. It was strange to be leading exercises instead of following Kiaran in them, but she was settling in. She winced a little when her dummies were first struck, but she knew the improved training results would be worth the effort and materials. The warband really was starting to look good. About halfway through the morning, she signaled to Geirny to sort everyone into sparring pairs, and the professionalism of their orderly rotation to a new exercise made her heart sing a little.

A bit before noon, though, a scream rang out across the valley, and then an answering cry, and Aesa started sprinting because an actual fight had broken out, and the center of the practice field had erupted into a mass of heaving and struggling bodies. Aesa and Nefja waded through the mess of elbows and flashing eyes and at last arrived at the epicenter where one woman, spitting invective, cradled her arm protectively to her chest. The target of her wrath struggled white-faced and trembling against the restraining hands of her friends. "Hold me baaack," Nefja sang quietly into Aesa's ear. Aesa shot her a look before stepping between the pair.

"What happened?" Aesa asked, and the resulting cacophony made her throw her hands up in the air for quiet. "Okay, talking stick, then," she said, grabbing a training baton and handing it to the closest person. What she could make out after discarding some of the more colorful language was that someone had gotten careless and hurt a bystander, that person had lashed out and was in turn struck again, some others had retaliated in defense of one or the other of the original combatants, and lots of people had opinions about who or what was to blame.

No one seemed very happy with Aesa's solution, which was to ask everyone to do their best to forgive each other and to resume practice. "Remember who our real enemy is," she said, and the resultant eye-rolling made her want to swallow her tongue. Snide remarks and dark glowers followed in her wake the rest of the session, and Aesa stewed in the injustice of it all until she could fling herself down at Cynisca's feet that afternoon.

"Won't you please come train these feral creatures?" she begged, but Cynisca remained impassive.

"Good time to learn to build trust," she said.

"What?" said Aesa, baffled.

"One of the best ways to learn something is to teach it," Cynisca replied, and refused to say more, although she communicated her displeasure with Aesa's defensive skills by inflicting several more bruises on her student's person.

The next day, Aesa suggested to the group that they begin their session with a prayer and a sacrifice to the gods. Responses ranged from tepid to sullen. Several of the youngest women actually broke ranks and captured the baby goat Aesa had brought for sacrificial purposes, so she flung up her hands and called it a wash. The warband seemed very pleased with its new frolicsome mascot, though.

It was evident that she'd need to try a different tack. Aesa let Geirny take the lead again during conditioning and ran with the corps. During partner sparring, Aesa lined up across from the trainee she considered to be weakest at the exercise: Dotta.

"So I'm seeing you struggle a little bit," Aesa said, smiling brightly to help take the sting out of her criticism. Dotta, bright-faced and scrubbed-looking under her helm, nodded.

"Well, it looks to me like you're slashing or trying to cut a little more than you're jabbing," Aesa said. "Obviously that's not going to work well with a baton, since there's no edge, but it's still not going to work well with an axe."

"I just don't want to hurt my partner," Dotta said, her voice trembling a little.

"Yeah, that makes total sense," Aesa said. "But in this case, it's your partner's job to keep you from hurting her." She flashed a sudden grin. "Obviously that's not a rule that applies anywhere else, really, but this one time it does. So we're going to spar, and I want you to really try and hit me; just really give me a good smack."

"All right," Dotta said, and walloped Aesa's weapon hand with a mighty blow that left Aesa near-breathless with pain.

"Yep," she said, pulling the injured arm behind her shield. "That was exactly right. Do just that. Good job." She jumped up and down a couple of times and took some deep breaths to help her frustration dissipate. Dotta looked worriedly at her face, and Aesa tried to smile reassuringly again. Later, though, when Cynisca tapped the same hand in afternoon practice, Aesa let out a shriek that startled the cat into the safety of the house.

"Take them over for me, won't you?" she begged. "You're so skilled that none of them can hit you, and I don't know if I'll make it through twice-lessons a day."

"You're developing those you lead," Cynisca said calmly. "Good job. I am developing you, though, so please move your head where I'm not going to hit it."

"Where's that?" Aesa asked.

"Away from my club," came the reply, and Cynisca launched into a furious onslaught that left Aesa feeling much more confident about the progression of her bob-and-weave skills, even if there was a bit of ringing leftover in her ears afterwards.

The next day, though, after there'd been a near-mutiny over wearing armor for the entirety of practice, her uncle lost patience with her.

"Please step in," Aesa had asked Cynisca, and Cynisca had said something about envisioning objectives, when they both jumped at the sound of wood clattering against wood. Martyn was banging two polished shapes together to get their attention.

"Aesa, is it really going to be every day with this?" he demanded. "You're wearing a groove in my ears."

Aesa shrugged, abashed. "I'm trying to be persistent."

"Yes, but think what you're being persistent about. Do you really want Cynisca to put herself in danger just so you don't have to improve your leadership skills?" Martyn said, his tone mild but his eyes dark.

"I mean, no," said Aesa. She glanced at Cynisca. "But do you really think you'd be in danger?"

"Why don't we trust her assessment," Martyn said. "It's her person she'd be risking."

"And yours," Cynisca said. She tucked her baton under her arm and patted Aesa's shoulder. "Sproutling, people often find difference frightening enough on its own. We don't farm all the way out here for no reason. Things . . . happened."

Her gaze flickered to Martyn's face, but Martyn had leaned back again, and his eyes were now firmly closed.

"I really think this group is different though," said Aesa. "I mean, I trust them with my life every day."

Cynisca smiled sadly. "Darling, your life may have different value to them than mine does. I know that may be hard to understand, but odds are someone in that group has parents among those who drove us out of the town. And those parents would be angry if they knew I taught their daughters to fight. I don't want to give them the excuse."

"I'm teaching them to fight. And Kiaran did before me. No one's come after us."

"Think about why that might be the case."

Aesa didn't really have to think about it. The caste system and its rules of order and honor, both spoken and unspoken, informed her actions every day. Her eyes welled up, and she recalled at last a thing she should have remembered before.

"Speaking of Kiaran, he's got at least a dozen thralls. Maybe now, while everyone's gone, it'd be a good time to, ah, free them." She felt absurd saying it to this suddenly austere woman, but at least she'd said it. Cynisca looked at her for a long moment before speaking.

"We talked about this, Aesa. Did you forget? The gods have bestowed on us a peculiar curse: that we are not truly free unless we have food, and the ability to get more." She sighed. "One man against several? They will have already thought about their situation, yes? And decided not to go at this time?"

Aesa blushed, and Cynisca laid a hand on her arm. "I don't mean to shame you, darling, but if they haven't left already, then there's something they lack. It may be money, like me, or weapons, or a workable plan, or something even more complicated. You won't know unless you ask them, and what will you do if you can't provide it?"

"Do you think it would be a bad idea to, uh, ask them?"

"I don't know. I'm not a thrall anymore, and I didn't speak for all thralls even when I was." A dozen emotions flitted across Cynisca's face. "Consider well the circumstance in which you approach them, if you do. That I do know."

ΦF

AESA'S THOUGHTS CHASED ROUND IN HER HEAD so much afterwards that she did not even remember the walk home. She knew when to visit Kiaran's farm to avoid him: early afternoon, since he would be anxious to begin hunting again, and generally took any excuse to visit the nearby woods after lunch. She considered approaching others for help, but somehow knew it wouldn't go well, especially before she knew what kind of help was actually needed.

It was therefore by herself that she slid down an embankment by Kiaran's back field, startling some nearby workers hauling tools. They glanced at her, took in her dirty-but-rich clothing, and resumed their progress like nothing untoward had happened.

Aesa brushed herself off and looked around. There was no sign of Kiaran, either in the fields or outside of his family's large house. The dark windows gaped at her, but remained empty for the long moments she inspected each in turn. Gnorri, Kiaran's mother, was largely bedridden. One never knew, though, if she was going to have a good spell. Before Aesa could feel too badly about wishing that today were not going to be one of those days, she forced herself over to the square where a number of women were doubled over, preparing neatly hoed rows for the critical spring planting.

"Um, hello," said Aesa nervously. A quiet, polite murmur answered her before silence reigned again. She watched the women for a few moments. Although some furtive looks were cast her way, they largely seemed committed to pretending she wasn't there.

It at last occurred to Aesa that her unmoving, upright stance would be identified immediately by an onlooker as being out of place, and she knelt on the far side of the woman working closest to the end of the row. She'd worn her drabbest dress, and she hoped it blended in well enough, color-wise. The fabric and cut alone evidently still marked her as different, and she wondered what other mistakes she'd made already.

No time for that. Aesa coughed quietly, and turned to the woman next to her.

"Would you like to leave?" she whispered gently. The woman, who had shown signs of confusion, now went stone-faced. "No, I'm very happy. Thank you."

Aesa blushed. "Sorry," she whispered. "It's not a trap. Kiaran hasn't sent me. I've got some money for you; I mean, it's not a lot, between you all, but you could get started. You could leave, if you wanted to."

"Leave?" a second woman said in a low voice that somehow carried even less than Aesa's whispers. "And how far would we get on your money before we were hunted?"

The first woman turned her back on the conversation and moved down.

"Maybe I could help you get away," Aesa said, casting an anxious glance at the first woman. "Maybe you could all start a farm, together . . ."

"What would we eat until autumn?"

"Uh, we're planning a raid on another clan. We could arm you, and you could lay claim to treasure. . . ."

The woman blew her breath out through her nose, dismissing the notion.

Aesa said hurriedly, "We're not just asking you to be another body. We've got enough. And we'd train you. You wouldn't go into battle untested."

The woman half-turned her face to Aesa, then winced and decided not to say whatever she'd been about to. "No, thank you."

She now clearly hoped Aesa would just go away, so accordingly Aesa moved along. She approached a third woman in the row, who hissed "No, thank you," before she even got close. The woman's face suddenly became fearful as a long shadow fell over them, but it still took Aesa a moment to recognize what was happening.

"Aesa? What are you doing?"

That was Kiaran's voice, imperious and angry in a way she'd rarely heard it. Aesa was suddenly more afraid of him than she had ever been, even in that torchlit dueling square. Her body ached at the absence of the weight of her axe, and she rubbed her right arm with her left as she straightened and turned to face him.

"Ah, I came to ask about their headwraps. Very practical, you see."

He seemed unmoved, so she added a flighty sort of gesture at her head and a shrug. "I had to know how they folded them." His darkened face cleared a little at her absurdity, but not entirely.

"Aesa, you're bothering them at work. Rather thoughtless of you, don't you think?"

"Yes, well, I couldn't find you, and I went looking, and got distracted. You know what I'm like." Her voice sounded high pitched and wild in her own ears, but Kiaran's frown was beginning to fade.

"Silly girl. I was over the ridge. Come to apologize, have you? You certainly took your time about it." He turned and walked towards the house, clearly expecting her to follow.

Aesa cast an agonized glance back at the thrall bondswomen, but they'd all turned to their work as if nothing had interrupted them in the first place. As she climbed the hill in Kiaran's wake, her eyes kept fixing themselves on the long knives strapped into his belt. She forced her gaze away and tried to think of happy things so her face wouldn't show fear. Ducklings. Rainbows. *Nothing bad is going to happen.*

Crossing the threshold of the great house, Aesa was blind in the dimness after the brilliance outside.

A reedy voice greeted her before she could locate its source. "Aesa! It's been too long since you were here. I hope you've come to sit a while."

Aesa's vision slowly adjusted until she could just make out a seated figure and a reclining one. The reclining figure finally revealed itself to be Kiaran's mother, Gnorri. From her place among the piles of cushions on the sleeping bench, she regarded Aesa with eyes that seemed to glow from within, like moonlit lamps. Gnorri raised a frail-looking arm from the coverlet to gesture at her companion.

"You know Mette, don't you? Such a nice girl, Mette."

Mette beamed cloyingly at Gnorri before turning a smile on Aesa that looked somehow as though she had a mouth full of blades.

"Mette's been helping Kiaran recover after his hunting accident," Gnorri continued. "My great bear of a boy is a fierce one, but he's awful at taking care of himself when he needs to."

"Relatedly, Aesa's come to apologize for her role in that hunting accident, mama," Kiaran said, smiling at Aesa.

Gnorri turned her moon-lamp eyes toward Aesa again. "Were you involved, then, Aesa? I must say, I find it shocking of you. The gods know how much I must rely on my dear boy, now that his father has gone." She sniffed, and Mette extended a comforting hand, which was gratefully clutched. "Was it necessary that you should hurt a mother's heart so?"

"Ah," Aesa said. Her mouth had gone dry. "I'm very sorry about the hurts I caused to Kiaran. And for your loss. Vigi was a great man."

"The greatest," Gnorri said, touching the back of the coverlet to her eyes. "We shall never see another like him. I will raise up a runestone to him that blots out the sun at noon. But one generation must make way for the next, I suppose, and this one shall rise to be even greater than his father, I hope."

Kiaran moved to his mother's side and touched her shoulder. His smile had not moved from his face. "Have no fear, Mother. When Aesa's father returns with the rest of our men, we will wreak vengeance for Father and everyone else hurt by our enemies."

Gnorri waved a hand irritably. "Blast Ottar for running off on his harum-scarum adventures, leaving his daughter to roam wild and dirty through the woods and get in your way."

Aesa glanced at her dress, which, admittedly, was rather dusty from kneeling in the soil. She brushed surreptitiously at it, causing Mette to make a small noise of disgust and spring up in search of a broom.

Gnorri clucked at Aesa. "What would your mother say if she could see you? Tangles in your hair, smudges on your face. You really must spend more time with us, Aesa. You need a mother's gentling influence. Why don't you start sitting with us in the afternoons? Mette cards wool as finely as you could wish, and I'm sure she'd be willing to teach you, if you promise to be a good pupil."

"It's a generous offer," Aesa said, "and of course I'd love to spend more time with you. But my afternoons are, ah, rather busy at present."

"Busy?" repeated Gnorri in evident confusion.

"Yes, Aesa, what can you have to be busy with?" Kiaran asked, his smile growing even broader. "You're practically landless, and you've no trade to occupy you. I'd think you'd be grateful for the opportunity to spend time with real ladies like my mother and Mette."

Aesa began to sidle away. "Very grateful for the offer, I'm sure," she said, squaring up with her back to the door. "But I've been helping Geirny with her work. Needs must, and all that. Now, if you'll excuse me, I promise I'll visit again soon. But for now, goodbye. Goodbye!"

She scuttled out as decorously as she could, followed by Mette's laughter and Gnorri's complaints. She was aware, without turning, of Kiaran's still-bright smile, and his eyes on her back as she hurried away down the path. The anxiety of the meeting would not leave her, and chased her through her dreams all that night.

In the morning, she discovered quite a rude phrase carved into the wood of her lintel, with related pictographs. She shivered, but could not quickly reach to obscure the graffiti, and since those women she knew with both more height and carving abilities would be at practice, she hurried away, hoping that no society matrons would inspect her house too closely that day.

Upon arriving at the playing fields, Aesa made a beeline for Geirny and tapped her on the shoulder. "Um, how quickly do you think we can be ready to go?" she asked, trying to seem nonchalant.

Geirny wasn't having it. "Go? Go where?"

"You know. Go," said Aesa, gesturing across the river.

"Oh, you mean, goooo," Geirny said.

Aesa nodded. "I've a notion that Kiaran means to try something."

"Something what?" Geirny asked.

"I don't know, precisely. But I brought myself to his attention again, and it didn't go well. If nothing else, he'll sic his mother on me. Óðinn knows she'd drive a dagger right through my heart if she knew I'd laid a hand on her precious boy."

"Kiaran's mother is no threat to anyone out of earshot," Geirny said. "You're the one who fought a duel over us needing more time. Why the hurry now?"

"It's just a feeling I have—," Aesa said, and the silvery thing in her chest leapt in agreement. "That it's time to go, or we shouldn't go at all. Look, the full moon's coming up, so it's perfect. We'll tell our mums that we're going to take a few days to go sing hymns to Freyja to bless the planting, and beseech her to send us husbands. They'll be thrilled that we're taking things so seriously."

"Are we taking things seriously?" Geirny asked. "This seems a bit rushed."

"I'm deadly serious. The question is if Kiaran knows that I am. I think he assumed that this whole thing fell apart without him, and once he realizes it hasn't . . ." Aesa trailed off, chewing at the inside of her cheek. "I can't say precisely what I'm worried about, but I feel like we need to move. And it's not like we're going to get much better."

She gestured at the orderly rows of focused, determined women preparing for the morning's exercises. "I'm saying let's get on the road before we can think too much about it."

Geirny stared at the training grounds, and at last sighed. "You're the leader, I guess," she said. "But getting an army on the march takes more than just saying 'go'. Don't be mad if it takes longer than you want to get us started."

It actually took far less time than Aesa expected. A lifetime of instruction in the art of being "game" mean that the women of her town could throw a picnic, a dance, or a clan festival together at a moment's notice. Assembling their disguises and carefully-prepared supplies for the raid in a limited time presented very little challenge at all.

"We had to beat out competition to the boys when we went to parties," Nefja reminded her when Aesa expressed amazement. "Gotta be ready quick!"

Dotta giggled as she hauled a bundle of supplies past them. "We don't even have to leave room in the schedule for getting pretty this time."

Geirny nodded. "We were always going to war," she said, smacking her axe handle soundly. "We're just bringing a different set of weapons this time."

"And our opponents aren't each other," Nefja added. "That'll be nice."

"I should assign a quartermaster," Aesa said. Nefja snorted. "Don't worry your head too much on that score," she said, tossing her head. "In any group large enough, there's bound to be one person who really loves telling everyone else How Things Should Be Done. I'll bet you a Byzantine *solidus* someone's already taken charge."

ΦF

NEFJA'S PREDICTION TURNED OUT TO BE ACCURATE. A bosom friend of Sigrun's who was usually in charge of organizing children's musicales was now applying her particular style of officious but kindly direction to everyone within range. Women stacked different kinds of supplies and tools in neat piles on the playing field. Runners darted back and forth between the staging area and the distant houses, retrieving forgotten items. Some mothers and aunts had even come to wave farewell, with tiny children peeping around their skirts.

"What do they think our axes are for?" Aesa wondered aloud.

"Bonfire," Dotta said. "Really big bonfire."

"And what'll we say if some of us don't come back?" Aesa asked.

"Tragically large bonfire," Nefja deadpanned.

The group formed up quickly of its own accord. Everyone was anxious to maximize the daylight and avoid the bad luck of night travel. Thus it was that before long, Aesa found herself at the head of a long column of women walking briskly alongside the still-snowy banks of the river to its closest fording. Upon arrival at the ford—

really just a narrowness between the two banks—everyone delicately picked their way across the icy logs that bridged the sparkling, chuckling death beneath their feet. One or two stepped poorly and found themselves instantly immobilized by the cold. Friends pulled them free of the river's grip and they had to exchange their footwraps for alternates from their packs while shivering from exposure, but by and large the squad made it across without major incident.

Past the black river and back on the frost-rimed forest tracks, the entire outing began to take on the tone of a sort of holiday, with women giving voice to snatches of songs they'd overheard from brothers and fathers. One brave soloist sang a lay she'd composed herself, while people improvised bits of harmonization around it.

Aesa sent a couple of scouts ahead—both to inspect the terrain, and to check for signs of life. She didn't want to hush the group and douse their good spirits, but the possibility of alerting their enemies to their presence unnecessarily meant the singing grated a bit on her nerves. They set up camp fairly early in the afternoon so they could begin the hunt for dry firewood with plenty of light to see by. They'd brought lots with them, but Geirny felt it was better to save that if possible. Aesa set up a watch and a cooking rota and generally fretted until the scouts returned, picking twigs out of their clothing. One raised a hand as she approached.

"Not much to report," the scout said. "The road's fairly clear, but doesn't show much use. No recent footmarks but ours. Don't worry, we kept our prints to a minimum," she said, forestalling Aesa's question. "From what I can tell, we won't be close to the settlement until at least tomorrow, so . . ." the second scout said with a shrug.

"So singing's all right tonight, then," Nefja said, hoisting her drinking horn happily. "We're supposed to be disguised as a party. We should be singing no matter what."

"'S long as it's you doing the singing," Geirny said. "Don't let Dotta solo; she sounds like a sick cat."

Dotta punched Geirny's arm. "Just because you don't appreciate my voice doesn't mean it's no good," she said, sticking her nose haughtily into the air. "You thought that bard who came through once was terrible too."

"Ooh, the one who did twenty verses of that saga? He was dreadful!" Geirny exclaimed. "No one liked him but Sigrun and her moony friends, and that's just because they liked his braids."

Aesa pulled her own braids round front and waved the ends about. "But he was oh, oh, so soooulful," she said, pretending to swoon into Dotta's arms. Dotta, overcome while trying to support Aesa's larger frame, staggered into Geirny, who almost fell over backwards before Nefja could catch her. The scouts backed slowly away until they were out of range of anyone's flailing limbs, then turned tail and ran for the nearest cooking fire.

Aesa sighed and composed herself. "Ought to go set some rabbit snares," she said, contemplating the huddled circles of humanity.

"Do you think you'll get any this early?" Dotta said. Aesa shrugged. "Doesn't hurt to try. Got to make sure Nefja doesn't eat all our rations on the first day." She winked, but Nefja still roared.

"Hey! It's you who has the bottomless stomach."

"Hence, I am going to try to catch some more food," Aesa said, bowing herself out. It was honestly good to be by herself for a little while. The shadows of the trees kept the snow from melting as quickly as it had in their home valley, and she found herself in a quiet dimness of ice and snow-covered leaves which required her to watch her step rather than think of what lay ahead. Her traps placed, she hurried back to the camp as the sun set over the ridge to discover that her bedroll had already been laid out for her by the largest fire. Ingirun sat next to it in her own bedroll, eating and studiously ignoring Aesa's gaze.

"Um, thank you," Aesa said to the air over Ingirun's head. There was no reply, so Aesa unpacked her own rations, removed her damp shoes, and sat with her feet as close to the fire as she dared.

By nightfall, neither had spoken. All around them, tall pines lanced into the star-filled sky—black, swaying shadows against a midnight backdrop. The camp's chatter had mostly died down, and Aesa was left chewing on the inside of her cheek, willing herself to speak so that Ingirun's gesture wouldn't go unappreciated. They could die tomorrow, after all, and at least Ingirun had made an overture. They lay on the ground like they often had together, heads propped on bedrolls, feet almost touching. It was all so familiar, with an undercurrent of strangeness that threatened to overwhelm her.

"Ingirun," she said, suddenly letting the name fly out into the air so she couldn't take it back. "Ingirun, that day of the *ping*. The Bride's Row, before we were raided. I feel . . . like if I could understand why you did it, I'd hate you for it less. I want to think you had a reason. I want to believe that our friendship—it was real, and it wasn't one-sided. But you knew what you were doing. You knew what it could do to my future, and you did it anyway. And you did it when you had everything coming—safety, wealth, love. So why, *why* did you try to take mine?"

Ingirun was silent. Aesa, in the agonizing moments that followed, decided that she was still glad she'd said it. The opportunity for truth-telling, even when met with lies or derision, was still worth offering. Probably.

The silence stretched on a little, and she began to contemplate the advantages and disadvantages of giving up her warm place near the fire so she could actually sleep, well, ever again, when Ingirun at last spoke.

"I did it because I had none of those things. Certainly not safety. And access to wealth, perhaps, but it would never be mine. I would never choose how to spend it. And I'd have to pay for it, every day, with access to my body. My foster father was negotiating access to my body with a man who I did not want to touch me, and no one asked me for permission!"

Her voice, rising from a whisper to a roar, evoked whimpers from nearby sleepers. Ingirun shook her head in disgust. "Marriage. Marriage, marriage, marriage—it's all we talked about, before. No, sorry, it's *getting* married that was the thing. We don't talk about what happens after, as though it isn't nice. And it probably isn't, for a lot of people. People who marry those who they don't want to touch. People who marry a person who makes their skin crawl, just so they can be safe, or eat."

Aesa felt a near-physical desire to struggle against Ingirun's words. "But we're told what happens to those who marry for lust. Their looks fade, and they grow dissatisfied. Better to marry for strength, or kindness—kindness lasts forever."

"But why not marry for all of it? Why not marry someone kind, whose touch you'd invite? Why not wait, until you can have both?"

"Because we can't," Aesa blurted.

"Why?" Ingirun said, her eyes near-glowing.

"You know very well."

"Say it."

You'd die, Aesa wanted to say, even though it wasn't technically true. Not being married only meant potentially losing your caste, and losing your caste wasn't actually dying. Thralls still lived. But they lived without choice, and they lacked anything to barter for it.

Except their bodies, if someone else wanted them. She shuddered, and she could see Ingirun guess where her thoughts had gone.

"There's a rude word that men and women consider a terrible insult for different reasons entirely," Ingirun said, lying back and turning her face to the sky. "Men use it when they want you to know that they have power, that they could literally buy your body from you if they wanted. Women use it against other women, because it's a thing they're afraid of. Or it's a thing they're afraid they cannot be, and that means they truly have nothing at all."

"We have our minds," Aesa said.

"But who will pay for a woman's mind?" Ingirun said. "A man, without strength, can still teach his sons the ways of war. What will they let us learn, against which we can barter when we're old? Why did they keep us from learning to fight?"

Aesa bit her lip before answering. "They don't want the competition when they're old men."

"Old men and old women are close to equal, in strength. An old man survives by knowing things of value."

"So do old women. All our teachers are old women!"

"And when was the last time you saw any of them wearing gold? And how many runestones stand testament to their lives? And what do they teach us?" Ingirun asked, clenching her fingers at her side. "How to be a good wife. They are paid in what we women can afford, and they can only live off of the little we give them at all because they all have husbands who add to their income. You never see a widowed teacher because she can't afford to eat off of what we can pay. So we're back to the beginning. It matters, very much, to be wifed. But if your life is not to be a misery of stifled fear every night, it also matters who you are wife to. And Kiaran, we thought, was tender and kind, and rich, and clever, and I did not mind the thought of him touching me. And in that he was rare, so I fought for him, as we fight for anything rare and valuable and important."

"As though we fought for our lives," Aesa said, sighing. She stared for a moment into the fire-dimmed brilliance of the stars above. "People might pay for your mind when you're old. You are a healer."

"If only I could bring myself to ask the dying for money," Ingirun said, smiling gloomily as she turned over to face Aesa again.

"You're such a squeamish woman."

"I am indeed squeamish."

The fire crackling behind them at last felt companionable, and the darkness through which the stars wheeled overhead did not seem so frightening to Aesa, even though their circumstances were no less strange. She wanted to say something chummy, to button their talk on a brighter note, or to let Ingirun know somehow that things would be all right. But Ingirun had gone to sleep in the intervening minutes, so Aesa merely smiled wryly into the vast night, and let tiredness claim her at last.

ΦF

SHE WOKE BEFORE DAWN THE NEXT DAY, and crept carefully out of the slumbering camp to retrieve her snares. Aesa nodded to the watch as she returned, empty traps slung over one arm, and found the squad just beginning to stir. Ingirun was absent from her bedroll by this time, and Aesa was more than a little glad. Midnight confidences didn't make for easy eye contact the next morning, and she had other things to worry about. Her mood seemed to infect the camp. People were jittery, or downright snappish with each other, and only birds sang that morning.

They trudged all that day through chilly woods—their combined frozen breaths creating a miniature sort of fog all around them. Uncomfortable quiet reigned after they left the constant babbling of the river behind, and Aesa couldn't decide which might be worse: facing death, or being cursed to walk through the gloomy grey dampness forever.

"At least death in battle might be quick," Nefja said upon being queried, "and we'd have the eternal honor of having been chosen for it by one *dís* or another." They bantered with each other for a bit until glares from their companions caused them to subside back into silence again.

It was therefore a great relief when Aesa spotted the disruption in their line from the scouts winding their way back towards her, and an even greater relief when she heard their report. Accordingly the group diverted themselves from the track, and by sunset found themselves huddled on a ridge with one of the Skjöldungar townships spread out before them. Smoke from its many fires collected in a haze above the dark dwellings, and Aesa shivered involuntarily.

"You're sure it's the right one?" she asked quietly, and one of the scouts nodded.

"I checked the totems on their picketed horses," she said. "The image is seared on my brain."

The second scout smiled grimly. "Feel free to double-check, though."

"No sign of our people, I'm assuming," Aesa said. Both scouts shook their heads, and Aesa nodded. "They wouldn't be allowed near the perimeter anyway. I'll look for them tonight."

"Tonight?" Geirny said, raising an eyebrow. "It'll invite some bad luck, won't it?"

Aesa shrugged. "I fear the spirits of the dead a little less than I fear the actions of the living if we're spotted camping here in broad daylight," she said. "I'd rather try for a little smash and grab than a pitched battle, yeah?" She heard no dissent, and having looked her fill, she half-climbed, half-slid inelegantly back down to the tiny valley they'd located in the hilly range that made up a sheltering wall of the Skjöldungar settlement.

Rage had started to fill her as she crouched there, and a desire to punish. She forced herself to take the sort of terribly deep, slow breaths that the wise women had made her practice over and over as a way of breaking out of negative feelings. And Óðinn knew she needed to break out of them, because indulging them and striking out at the first Skjöldung she met wouldn't make for a successful mission. But oh, how good it felt to just imagine the roar she'd let loose, and the way they'd cringe and promise to make amends as she brandished her weapon at them.

"Are you all right?" Dotta asked, and Aesa shook her head to clear it of her reverie. Under Sigrun's direction, the women were preparing their campsite for a long and fireless night—arranging bedrolls into neat, tightly packed squares with periodic aisles in between. "I'm not sure I'm even going to be able to sleep tonight," Dotta admitted, following the direction of Aesa's gaze.

"You're welcome to come with me, if you like," Aesa said, grinning. Dotta shook her head vehemently. "No thank you. One stranger will be hard enough to conceal."

"I wonder about that," Aesa said. "Wouldn't a pair of women seem even more innocuous than a lone, furtive-looking one? Or at least less likely to attract the attention of a bored man?"

Dotta considered it, but shook her head again. "One unfamiliar face probably won't create alarm in someone's brain, but two might set someone to wondering. Wondering leads to comment, which leads to questioning, which leads to danger. I mean, more danger than you'll already be in," she said, looking Aesa over anxiously. "Plus I only carved enough totems to outfit one person. And speaking of, you'd better get your outfit on while we can still see to get everything pinned and painted properly."

So it was that Aesa found herself slipping into the alien, torch-lit avenues of the town, arrayed in her blandest gown, with Skjöldung shield-and-sheaf brooches firmly fastened at throat and hip and in her braid. Fortunately the streets were largely empty, so hopefully her minimal disguise would not be put to much scrutiny. She clutched a large water skin by way of visual explanation for her presence outside of the home on such a forbidding night, and willed her face to look placid. It was more of a struggle there, in the actual moment, than she'd ever imagined, since not only was she walking through enemy territory, but a wealth of the wise womens' lectures on walking alone at night had chosen that moment to resurface in her mind.

You'll be an easy target.

You'll appear of easy virtue.

The dead resent the living intruding upon their roaming time.

Aesa shivered, then forced herself to smile at a passing elder who looked at her in concern. The resulting lack of challenge shocked some confidence into her heart, and she proceeded more boldly down the narrow streets, glancing down each alley for some sign of her captured kinsmen. She discovered that the town was organized on roughly the same lines as her own, allowing for the variation in terrain. If her father had been more given to taking captives, she might have guessed herself where their people might be held. As it was, she found herself making some rapid visual assessments. The buildings among which she currently walked were not richly carved, but were still too grand to house thralls. She began to work her way downhill, banking on the idea that Skjöldungar farmers would likely have the same intention as her own people to channel snowmelt into their fields, but that the consequent occasional flooding would make housing at the base of the mountain benches less desirable.

Her guess proved to be correct. The solid, well-built houses of the hills gave way to ruder structures shored up in places by earthworks, and as she cautiously proceeded, even those lowly buildings were replaced by muddy pit hovels. The wailing cry of a small child escaped from the chinks in one house, but the sound choked off after a couple of cracking slaps. Aesa winced, and paused irresolutely outside of the house for a moment before shaking herself and hurrying on. Another noise caught her attention: the slurred shouts of a group of bravos out on a night's revelry. She quickly dodged around a corner into a dank, smelly alleyway to avoid them.

As she glanced around to determine her next move, she found her eye drawn to a heartbreakingly familiar symbol: the dim outlines of a rearing bear, carved crudely and hastily into a log of the wall opposite. Her hand reached out of its own accord, and she found herself tracing the shallow chips in the wood with a pained reverence. She closed her eyes, pulled herself together, and started examining the wall's surface for weaknesses. Her questing fingers found several; the mortar between logs was old and crumbling, and her heart ached for the way the chill must seep through the chinks on a windy night. Enlarging a particularly promising hole took more than a few anxious moments, though. She scanned the muck around her feet for something to dig with, but could not bring herself to feel through the sludge with her hands. Filth on her clothing could draw attention anyway, so she settled for carefully probing the edges of the hole with a fine-bladed dirk she'd concealed on her person—praying she wouldn't accidentally stab someone.

When at last her dagger met with no more resistance, she peered through the self-made opening in the wall, but either the building was empty of inhabitants, or they'd not been granted any kind of light. Aesa glanced over her shoulder, and risked leaning around the corner of the building to look both ways down the path again before cooing softly in what she hoped was a reasonable imitation of a quail. It was too early for quail, but she couldn't think of a more tactical sound to make, and she needed her call to carry at least a little way into the darkness of the hovel, especially in case someone slept within.

Her heart nearly stopped when she heard a ragged answering call. She plastered herself against the wall, took a deep breath, and whispered, "Clanfriend?"

There was no response, so she tried again, a little more loudly. "What clan?"

"Bjǫrn, and none better under the winter sun," came a harsh whisper, and Aesa sagged against the cold wall in relief.

"It's Aesa Ottarsdóttir," she whispered, pressing her cheek against the wood so she could speak and watch the alley entrance at the same time.

Another voice spoke at the gap. "Aesa? This is Hrefna, Ingirun's foster mother. Don't come to the door; it's barred on the outside and we're watched from across the way."

Aesa found herself nodding in response, even though Hrefna couldn't see her. "I haven't come alone. There's a squad up the ridge. Are you all together? Is there anyone more I should seek out?"

There was a brief silence, during which Aesa clenched her jaw and tried not dance with impatience until Hrefna finally spoke.

"Most are with us. Some were taken from us that first day, and we haven't seen them since."

Flooded by grief, Aesa tilted her head back to gaze at the night sky, and silently prayed for inspiration about what to say. No help was immediately forthcoming.

"Well, I've found most of you, and that's a blessing," she said at last. In her daydreams they'd triumphantly gotten everyone home again. She forced herself to focus. "When is the best time to spring you, do you think?"

There was a silence again. When Hrefna's voice came at last, it was tinged with weariness. "I'm not sure you should, Aesa. Our clan can ill-afford to lose any men you've brought with you, and . . ."

"I can guarantee that we will not lose a single man to your rescue," Aesa said dryly. "But you've been here, so you know their patterns, and . . ." She broke off when she realized that some sort of scuffle was taking place behind the wall, and the first voice hissed at her through the gap.

"I'll tell you whatever you want to know. If you're willing to help, I want to try to get out of here. I've seen the bond markets, and I'll summon whatever faith and courage is necessary to avoid them."

"You'd let someone die for your freedom?" Aesa heard Hrefna ask, and in the silence following, Aesa imagined she could hear the other woman's glare. Aesa coughed.

"It is our choice, and would be our honor," she said. "We've worked long and hard to be ready for this. What can you give me by way of strategy?"

The first voice came again, more strongly. "We're roused at dawn, ordinarily, and we work until sundown, and there's a light guard but the farms are far away from the main town, so a force could take it down without too much fear of backup arriving quickly. I've a red kerchief, still, and Sveni's got an ugly blue shirt they didn't take, so you can find us since most everyone else wears brown."

The voice faded away a little at the end as the speaker turned to confer with others in the room. "Is there anything else she needs to know?"

"Tell her we're at the second east-most plot and it's got three story stones on the right side," Aesa heard Sveni say, and she couldn't help but smile joyfully at hearing his reedy voice again.

"We'll come for you," Aesa promised. "If not this morning, for some reason, then soon. We won't stop trying to save you." Tears pricked her eyes, and she brushed them away impatiently, trying to steel herself for the walk back.

The whispers from the hole in the mortar nearly undid her as she finally pulled herself away: "We love you, Aesa. We'll see you soon. Thank you."

Now it was time to contain the sadness and the rage, or at least keep them from her face. She thought about snow bears, and steel, and stone. She tried to force her fingers to relax on the waterskin. At least holding it kept her from curling her hands into fists. She was almost a third of the way back to the place where a tiny, rough path would lead to the shadowy trail back to her camp when a hand closed on her shoulder. She bit back a scream.

"What, you didn't hear me calling to you?" the hand's owner, an older man with a giant, spittle-marked beard, said. Aesa thought he meant to be playful, and tried to look amused instead of terrified.

"I didn't, I'm sorry. I'm focused on getting home."

"I'll come with you. It's not safe for you to be that pretty and walking around so late." He waggled his eyebrows at her, and Aesa nearly retched with stress.

"No, thank you, I'm nearly there." She nodded to him—even managing a smile—and began to move on, but he merely wheeled and started to walk up the hill beside her.

"So it won't take me much out of my way, then." He held out his elbow, and she ignored it, although she couldn't help worriedly glancing at his face to see if the refusal had made him angry. He settled for reaching up and lifting her hair away from the nape of her neck to examine the forgotten Ingwaz rune that Geirny had painted there for luck.

"That's beautiful," he said, even as she leaned away. "What's it for?"

"Beginnings," she said, trying for a tone of polite unfriendliness.

"Beginnings!" he repeated happily, her tone evidently uncommunicative. "Auspicious for me, then, wouldn't you say?"

Aesa smiled thinly and picked up her pace, hoping a fast uphill climb might discourage this giant of a man more than her outright declining of company had.

He puffed a little, but did not seem immediately dissuaded. "So, do you have runes . . . anywhere else on your body?"

Fear curdled fury in her heart, since even if she stabbed this man outright, his shouts of pain would likely wake at least one curious person. No one in this night-drenched quarter of shadowy doorways was on her side, even supposing she could hit something vital through his enveloping furs.

"Just that one," she said evenly, no longer even facing him as she spoke.

"Oh, come on, now, girly," he pressed, squeezing her elbow, and fury, with a roar, at last broke the ice of her fear.

"Do not touch me," she hissed, and fear reclaimed her in its frozen grip as first shock, then shame, then anger swirled over the man's face. His eyes darkened, and he swung his hand up but inspiration struck first, and she stepped back and blurted, "I'm ill. I'm ill, and the wise woman says those who touch me will get ill too, so you don't want to touch me again."

He recoiled from her, then gathered his dignity. "Oh. Well, you should have told me, girly, when I offered you my arm."

"I should have," Aesa said. "I'm sorry. I must get home, though, you see."

"Yes, get you home," he said, huffily waving a hand at her. He turned, shaking his head and muttering to himself, and Aesa forced herself to move, but not break into a flat-out run. Every sound from the shadows made her flinch, though, and the sour feeling in her stomach did not abate until she found herself surrounded again by the scrubby hill trees which marked one edge of the enemy town.

She sent a silent thanks winging skyward for escape, and for the brilliance of the moon that lit her way. When she at last stumbled into camp, she actually managed to grin a little, for Sigrun's aisles had been muddled over with bodies striving even in sleep to not remain on the chilly edges of the formerly neat squares. Even while she watched, several women mushed themselves closer together. Dotta, crouched on a rock with her bedroll folded under her, nodded an anxious greeting.

"Found them. We'll need to move at dawn," Aesa said quietly. Dotta's answering smile was bright in the moonlight, and she startled Aesa by leaping off of her perch and enfolding the other woman in a fierce hug.

Aesa reflexively flinched a little, and Dotta sprang away again, her eyes wide with concern. "I'm sorry," she whispered. "I should have . . ."

Aesa gave her a quick shake of the head, and a reassuring smile. "You have my permission to hug me whenever you like," she said. "I've just been on guard. You know the feeling."

Dotta nodded, and glanced at her erstwhile guard post. "I need to remember to ask, though. Not everyone's glad of hugs." She sighed a little. "Nefja always reminds me I'm too much of a cuddleworm."

Aesa snorted despite herself. "Nefja's the biggest cuddleworm of all," she said, gesturing down the hill to where Nefja's sleeping form could just be glimpsed in the center of a pile of people. "Think she got there by accident?"

Dotta made an outraged face, then grinned and yawned hugely. Aesa pulled Dotta's bedroll off of the stone and handed it to her sleepy friend. "I'll finish your watch," she said. "I'm not likely to be able to sleep for a bit after all the excitement."

The other woman nodded gratefully, and trudged down the slope. Aesa watched Dotta try to negotiate her way into a warm spot without actually waking anyone, before sitting and leaning back to watch the stars whirl overhead until she was at last relieved of her post.

ΦΡ

THE FIRST OBVIOUS FLAW IN AESA'S PLAN turned out to be her route down to the farmsteads. A warband makes noise—even one trying to be stealthy—and theirs was not particularly quiet, given the saturated ground they were trying to squelch their way over.

They'd heard cracking noises, like rocks knocking together, but couldn't locate their origin, so they'd shrugged and moved on until the snow beneath their feet suddenly slid away, and what looked to Aesa's terrified eyes like half of the mountainside went tumbling past. Boulders the size of cows hurtled down the slope, smashing trees and smaller stones in their wake, but the roaring and implacable sheet of grey-white snow that carried those boulders along did more damage itself than Aesa could possibly have imagined. The members of the warband snatched and clung to exposed roots for safety, but many anchors proved slippery and treacherous amidst the icy onslaught.

A second slab of snow cracked, and a billowing mass of fog enveloped the band. Aesa squeeezed her eyes shut against the gritty powder, trying to keep the terror of finding herself suddenly blind, deaf, and helpless from overwhelming her. She braced herself against the mountainside, aware that at any moment her feet could be swept out from under her, and counted the seconds until the roaring died down and she could bring herself to open her eyes again.

After the last monstrous sounds faded away, there came a dreadful silence. Then a quiet weeping made itself heard, for more than one woman had nearly been carried away entirely by the earth's tumult.

Aesa, who had been towards the back helping those whose feet had mired in the soggy ground, stood very still as dozens of pairs of eyes turned to her, filled with expressions as varied as the faces of their owners. She tried to put her own terror and grief aside, and assume a calm mask. She wasn't sure how convincing her expression really was.

"Is this a judgment from the gods?" someone asked quietly.

Aesa looked upslope, at the mountain's newly scarred face, and bit her lip. "I don't think so," she said in a low but carrying voice. "Ingirun's the closest thing we have to a shaman, though. What do you think?"

Ingirun pursed her mouth. "You already know what I think. It's no judgment, just a fact." She sighed and turned to help Nefja undertake a rapid head count. The rest of the women calmed one another, though some flinched at each fresh sob. The mountain's quiet was now as vast and remorseless as had been the scale of destruction, but would it remain so?

In muted tones, Aesa instructed the warband to turn the line. She checked in with those nearest her, but there seemed little question of relinquishing their mission. Single-file, in resolute but wary silence, they slowly picked their way back across the trail and down across a different, gentler set of slopes until they came nearly to the walled edge of the Skjöldungar township itself.

Here scrub trees meant to keep the red deer from foraging in Skjöldung gardens kept the soil from slipping, but would provide scant cover for the warband as they made their way from the town's main gates to the work fields.

"So, what, we're supposed to hope they don't look up?" Nefja whispered, wrinkling her nose at the intermittent cover between the foothills and the buildings.

Aesa shrugged. "That's about it," she admitted. "Unless you've a better idea. But it's not exactly like anyone's going to look at us and think, 'That's an invading army, that is.'"

"Well, they should," Dotta said stoutly, and Geirny grinned.

"So they should," she echoed, "so we must do our best to not look like one."

They did so by making their way across the length of the town in scattered clumps of three and four, chatting quietly and trying hard to radiate a leisurely unconcern. One woman in Aesa's group seemed inclined to want to whimper, but when it was their turn to go, squared her shoulders and quite startled her sworn leader by being able to sustain a bright conversation about animal husbandry all the way to the apple orchards that separated the town from their target steadings. When they were safely past the town, she plumped down on the chilly earth and tucked her head between her knees, sucking in great lungfuls of air. She waved off concerned hands, though, and even managed a grim smile at Aesa as she rose, brushing dirt from her clothing.

It was while Aesa anxiously watched the final groups make for the cover of the trees that she realized where things could have gone wrong. Her face blanched, and she exhaled slowly as the last women darted into the mazy green-grey tunnels formed by the budding trees.

"What is it?" Geirny asked, and was startled by Aesa's turning a face full of hilarity to her.

"Wrong outfits for idle strolling," Aesa choked out.

Geirny blinked, and looked over the warband, and it slowly dawned on her that yes, the troop of women with their long braids, smooth faces, mannish trousers, and bristling weaponry would have seemed highly incongruous to an onlooker, but that long days of training had made the sight seem perfectly normal.

"I always hate it when I wear the wrong dress for the occasion," Sigrun sighed mournfully. "Ah, well. We'll just have to murder any men who see us." She began to stroll off, humming a cheerful tune half under her breath.

"Not Sveni," Dotta called quietly after her.

"All right, not Sveni, and not Nefja's brother. But any non-Bjǫrn shall die for the sin of having looked upon our glory."

Aesa and Geirny gaped after her.

"Woman knows how to make an exit," Geirny admitted.

Aesa shook her head in admiration. "Onward, then."

The second flaw in Aesa's plan involved the farmsteads themselves. Although she'd heard Sveni's direction of second-most eastward, it hadn't really sunk in that Skjöldung farms might have a vastly different layout than Bjǫrn fields, since the towns were so similar. But where their territory forced farmers to space themselves out like silver beads on a string, here a warm, friendly current meant that snow barely touched the wide farming plains, and they sat cheek by jowl in a close patchwork.

Aesa had prepared tactical teams to attack along the edge of a farm, but the guards patrolling both the edge and centers of the elongated rectangles meant that some groups might to have to rush over a very large open space indeed to keep their intended quarry from killing their loved ones.

For loved ones there were, in that open space. Sveni's blue shirt mocked the grey early morning sky with its brightness as he bent over a nearly-tilled row. A woman in a scarlet kerchief knelt not far from Ingirun's foster mother. Nefja stopped breathing for a moment at the sight of her brother, then begged Aesa to task her with scouting an alternate route for retreat, or anything else to keep her occupied for a few minutes so she didn't just sit and think of calling out to him. Aesa motioned for her to go, and glanced around quickly to see if anyone else was similarly distressed. Looking at the grim, set faces, she summoned her own resolve and tried to rework her strategy.

But as she stared at the guardsmen from the treeline, trying to detect the pattern in their patrols, her sense of them traitorously shifted. One was older than her grandfather had been when he died. Another, warming chilled hands near a small fire, was barely older than Sveni. These men had friends, and likely family too. She'd sworn her warband to try to disable rather than kill—to damage, not destroy—but her hope that no one would die lay faint in her chest.

She queried the silvery feeling that had so often prompted her. *Is this really the right thing to do?* There was no response. Then she saw one burly guard shift and lay his hand meaningfully on the hilt of his bearded axe. A woman had sat down to rest, but at the gesture, slowly turned herself over and began her toils again.

Right. These were not just men, but men who hit. Men who beat others to control them. Men who enslaved because it was less resource-expensive for them than paying workers. An image of Kiaran and his father flitted through her mind, and she shuddered. Enough introspection.

Nefja returned to Aesa's side, shaking her head. "The way up the hill leads back to the mudslide, I think, and we obviously can't cross that at speed."

Aesa bit her lip. "Back the way we came, then," she said grimly. "Pick a reserve team out to be rearguard."

"How do you want to go in?" Dotta asked, her anxiety and her determination equally evident on her face.

"The way of our fathers," Aesa said. "Shock, overwhelm, and retreat." She rattled off assignments to the women surrounding her, who repeated them to those further away. Heads nodded to Aesa in understanding, and the designated captains of each team raised a silent hand to confirm acceptance of their role. One, and then more of those hands reached down, to those women next to them, and Aesa found herself linking hands with Dotta and Geirny on either side, suddenly part of a living chain of affection. The fragility of it all brought Aesa to tears, but she could not wipe them away, for that would mean releasing hands that she might never hold again.

"Þórr will guide our axes, and Óðinn receive the slain," she said at last, and gestured for the attention of her teams. Upon receiving each of the captain's nods and their ritual whisper: *We are ready to fight, and ready to die if chosen*, she motioned them all to move out.

The first two men fell silently, mobbed at the edge of the forest by teams of five women deploying axe handles to throat, feet, and shoulders. A third raised a hoarse shout to alert others, and in response the Bjǫrn women burst forth from the underbrush with bloodcurdling wails, streaking across the field to meet startled opponents.

Sveni and others leapt for their own captors, clutching at arms and weapons in the hopes of preventing retaliatory strikes against the unarmed workers. Aesa dashed the butt of her axe into the neck of a warrior who was striking out at prisoners as he tried to free his blade hilts from their grasping fingers. He went down after a solid thump from Sigrun, and Sveni goggled at them both.

"I didn't expect you'd come yourself," he gasped as he snatched up the fallen guard's axe and belt knife, stepping a little unnecessarily on the man's arm. She grinned broadly at him, then sprinted to where Dotta was trying to chivvy another prisoner into moving. Despite the fighting around them, the kneeling woman's compressed lips and tightly-folded arms indicated a certain amount of distrust.

"We are trying to rescue you," Aesa heard Dotta say impatiently as she and Sveni caught up. "Please be rescued."

"Or not, and we'll leave you with this lot," Aesa said, jerking her head at an onrushing pair of furious guards. "Up to you." She smiled a little as the woman at last clambered quickly to her feet.

Sigrun engaged the closest of the warriors, ignoring Sveni's indignant squawk about it. Aesa waited for the second warrior to come to her. As he closed, she snarled directly into his face before pivoting off of her front foot, unfolding her arm and using the momentum to strike at the man's exposed shoulder.

He staggered out of the reach of Aesa's blade, but promptly had his legs swept from beneath him by Dotta's well-aimed kick, and their enemy fell at Nefja's feet as she arrived, half-hauling Magnus, her brother, who was bleeding profusely from the side of the head.

"Don't fuss overmuch, Dotta; scalp wounds bleed like anything," she said breathlessly to her dismayed-looking friend. Magnus nevertheless managed a grateful smile to Dotta as she hurriedly bound his head with a bandage from her pack and stood on her toes to knot it securely.

Behind them, Geirny limped by with her arms joyfully clasped around her mother, forcing Aesa to tear her eyes away from the gore and recall her duties.

"Have we rounded ours up?" she asked Nefja, scanning the field. Two or three clumps still battled with opponents, but a stream of people were already running for their designated regrouping spot.

"Near as I can tell," Nefja said. "I don't want to stick around for too much of a head check though. We've already engaged far more guards than we thought we would."

Aesa nodded and, raising her fingers to her lips, whistled sharply to signal the retreat. She glanced anxiously at the far fields before turning to run herself, snatching up a brand from the guards' firepit on the way. "Sveni, you don't know of another way out, besides through the orchards, do you?"

He shook his head, pursing his lips in concern.

"They've never led us anywhere else," offered a woman running behind them. "Unless you have boats. Then we could . . ."

Aesa shook her head. "We came overland," she said shortly. "We'll go the hard way. More honor in that anyway, yeah?"

"More something," Sveni said, shaking his head again, and then shouts were heard at the town gates and conversation ceased in favor of an all out sprint through the orchard.

The third flaw in her plan, Aesa thought as she hurdled treacherous roots and dodged low branches, was not resetting after she'd observed the first flaw. Backtracking had cost them an early enough start, which meant that now, during their retreat, the ordinary people of the township were beginning to stir and go about their day. Some already clustered menacingly in the gaps of the rough walls that served as gates for the unfortified town, while others ran for help. Aesa held the flame of her brand to some of the driest-looking walls as her friends sprinted past, but could only hiss through her teeth until she at last got a patch of rushes to catch.

Nefja, far ahead, had caught on to the plan and was attempting to fire the far gateposts, her brother leaning over to blow frantically on the reluctant fuel. By the time Aesa caught up, some town guards were indeed beating at the licking flames, but others were pursuing their escaping prisoners. Their furred boots churned the damp ground, and Aesa felt nearly hypnotized by the decrease in the gap between pursuer and pursued. The prisoners were clearly unused to running after their enforced confinement and most looked agonizingly slow. Geirny and others were doing their best to encourage them along, but the men chasing them had long, bright blades and longer strides . . .

"Hey!" The yell tore from Aesa's throat before she was fully conscious of forming it, and she tried again more strongly. "Hey!"

Three men of the seven turned to look behind them, and upon spotting the source, two peeled off to pelt towards her, their faces full of venom and frustration. The frustration increased when she darted up the slope of the foothill, forcing them to chase her up steep terrain where a loose stone underfoot could cause a turned ankle or worse. Pausing for the briefest of instances to check the best path for ascent, Aesa snatched up a rock and hurled it with all her might at them before resuming her frantic climb. She smiled in grim satisfaction as a pained grunt and a pebbly sliding noise confirmed at least one success, but was forced to hike blindly for a moment as her attention was claimed by a dark figure waving at her furiously from a hill off to her right. Aesa couldn't make out what Ingirun's repeated miming meant until the first arrow whistled over her head and she had to duck, late but instinctively.

She hunched her shoulders tightly and tried to dart in an erratic non-pattern across the dew-slick slopes. A second arrow embedded itself in the hillside to her left, but she thought if she could just make it back to the sparse cover of the leafless deer trees, her pursuers' arrows and spears might be more likely to rattle harmlessly off of the entangling branches than find their target. It was therefore with a little surprise that she found her progress halted by the sudden blooming of jagged pain through her back, and noted Ingirun's anguished scream. Her breath, what she could get of it, was excruciating and shallow, and she found herself pitching forward as the earth of the grey hill rushed up to meet her. A blackness roared over her mind then, a mercy as it were, since she did not feel the final bite of the warrior's blade as it arced mercilessly into her prone body.

PART TWO

ᚠᚠ

Consciousness burst back over her, and she felt herself weight-less, but strangely not sightless, even though she understood quite clearly that her body was now somehow below the rest of her. She saw Ingirun try to run to her, only to be caught up by Nefja and Geirny's restraining arms. She grasped reflexively at her killer's form as he turned to pursue her friends, but she no longer had a form to grasp with, and it was Dotta who darted back to meet his charge. Grim and tearstained, she hurled herself forward into range. Where they met, weapons flashed and blood spurted, but before Aesa could identify whose blood it was, she felt another wave of onrushing darkness and could see no more.

The next time Aesa awoke, her friends were gone. Her body was also missing, birdsong again filled the hillside, and two women stood in the air before her—one pale, rather like a more statuesque Sigrun, and the other dark of skin and hair. Clad in gowns not un-like those Aesa herself owned, their clothing nevertheless had an air of refinement likely unreplicable by her village's most skilled tailors. These must be the fabled *dísir*, she thought—an idea that flooded her with joy for a moment—but why was there more than one? She frantically tried to decide which fact to address first, but the pale one spoke, halting her rumination.

"I am here to extend to you an offer of welcome to Fólkvangr," she said with a smile. Aesa's mind noted that the smile did not look entirely comfortable. Unnerved, she shifted her gaze to the curly-haired woman, who also smiled, but in a wry sort of way.

"I'm sorry for the pain you've just experienced," she said in a rich alto. "And for the strangeness you might feel at the loss of your body. If you're like me, you'll be feeling off for a while, but it fades, mostly. I'm Kára, and I would like to offer you welcome to Valhǫll, and also to answer all of your questions, once you've chosen."

Aesa frankly felt overwhelmed by the number of questions she had, as well as by the suspected impact of the choice she was asked to make. "You won't answer my questions before?"

"Can't, really," said the pale woman, and Kára also shook her head. "I'm bound by honor to not try to influence your decision too much," she said. "It is for you only to decide between Valhǫll and Fólkvangr. You will know what is right."

Aesa tried not to snort. Following her heart had gotten her into this mess. "Seems awfully unsporting, though," she finally managed to say.

Kára nodded, but the other woman simply looked impatient.

Sorry my giant decision is taking a moment, Aesa thought irritably, and tried to dig in her metaphorical heels. "What if I didn't choose, yet?" she asked. "Can't I just, I dunno, wander the earth or something for a while?"

"No," said the pale woman.

Again, Kára was more forthcoming. "Your spirit feeds from its connection to a godly power," she said. "Your own strength is not enough to sustain it right now. Without choosing, you will dwindle away into nothingness."

Aesa, her sense of anxiety growing as she realized she was in fact feeling a little blurry around the edges again, looked quickly from face to face. "Can I ever leave, once I've chosen?" she asked a little desperately.

"Yes," said Kára, but "No," said the other. Kára looked at the pale woman sharply, but she remained unmoved.

"No," she simply repeated meaningfully, looking into Kára's eyes. Kára's lip curled a little, but she said nothing.

"All right, it's obvious, then. I choose Valhǫll," Aesa said. Kára instantly broke out into a broad smile, and she offered her hand, but the other woman was undaunted.

"Are you sure?" she asked, her face suddenly sorrowful.

"No, but a fat lot of help you've been about it," Aesa said.

The woman's lips tightened slightly, but she reached out her hands beseechingly. "We have endless feasting and mead and a host of earthly delights. Won't you reconsider?"

"I've heard Valhǫll has all those things too," Aesa said, looking to Kára for confirmation.

"Something like," Kára agreed. "Feasting and delights, certainly, and we're happier than these icicles can ever be!" She delivered that last directly to the other woman's astonished face, and Aesa chuckled despite herself.

"Spiteful!" she cried, and Kára grinned, only slightly abashed. "I'm working on it," she said.

The other woman coughed, and said smoothly, "If you change your mind, ask her where to find us. Freyja will always open her door to you."

Aesa squinted at this. "I thought you said . . ." she began, but the woman merely turned as though to walk away, somehow fading from Aesa's sight at the same time. Aesa blinked reflexively as the afterimages danced in her vision.

Kára, unfazed, reached out her hand again, and Aesa took it. At least she thought she had, but she did not sense it. No warmth exuded from the other woman's palm, nor did Aesa feel pressure from where Kára's fingers appeared to clasp her own.

"Ready?" Kára asked. Aesa shook her head. "Have you chosen other women here? Do you know if my friends are all right?"

Kára frowned sympathetically, her eyes suddenly sparkling with tears. "I do not know the fate of your friends. You may be able to seek them out," she said. "But for now, you must make your own connection to the All-Father. I can sustain you myself for only a little while."

"Where must we go to do that?"

"Ásgarðr," came the reply. "Home of the gods and your ancestors. Are you ready now?"

"No," said Aesa. "But let's go anyway."

Kára closed her eyes, and the two were suddenly surrounded by a great darkness. Aesa's mind tried frantically to determine the origin and scope of her feeling of speed, until she finally realized that the streaks passing her by might in fact be stars. They stopped almost as suddenly as they started, and Aesa tried instinctively to catch her breath while taking in her surroundings.

She was not to be particularly successful at either endeavor. One, she no longer breathed at all, and two, the vastness of the space in which she stood defied all measurement. Soaring archways led off in all directions from a huge hall made of some kind of glowing stone.

On some of the walls between hung rich tapestries depicting lush gardens full of intricately embroidered foreign plants and sparkling streams so finely rendered that Aesa half expected the water to burble at her on its course. In front of her, almost strangely, stood a pair of doors of a very ordinary scale compared to their surroundings. Made of carved lindenwood, from what Aesa could tell, they beckoned with a sort of friendliness, and Aesa gestured at them.

"Is that where I'm supposed to go?" she asked.

Kára nodded. "Do you feel ready?"

"To meet the All-Father? Does anyone?"

"Do you?" Kára asked seriously, her eyes searching Aesa's face.

"How much time do I have if I don't?"

"Not a whole lot. Time works a little differently here, and just being so near helps. But enough to compose yourself, if you'd like."

Aesa glanced around, although every place her eye alighted threatened to draw her attention for hours. There was nowhere to sit, and muted sounds from beyond the archways suggested a lack of privacy beyond. She thought about asking Kára for a room or an alcove or something, but discovered to her surprise that if she merely closed her eyes, the sense of everything else faded away—even the faint undercurrents of noise.

Here, then, in the privacy of her own mind, she considered her life. She thought of early squabbles with her family, and humiliations experienced in front of and by the hands of her peers. Sigrun's face appeared in her mind, as did Ingirun's and Kiaran's. Thinking of Kiaran reminded her of her intense longing to change her world, starting with her hoped-for family. She thought of her acute frustration over the way her people wielded weapons against each other, and her rage over the apparent necessity of those weapons to defend against outsiders. She thought of her own willingness to take up arms herself. She thought of her treatment of Martyn, and Cynisca, and her friends' servants. She thought of the way the exposed throat of the warrior looked as she'd clubbed an axe handle into it.

Aesa opened her eyes and shrugged at Kára. "I'll feel like a peeled bug no matter what, I think," she said. "Can't change that. Might as well face things."

Kára smiled a little wryly, and looked as if she wanted to speak. Instead, she reached for the door's handle. The door swung silently open, and even more light spilled out, gleaming from the revealed space.

Aesa tried to take a deep breath, made a face, bobbed her shoulders minutely at Kára, and stepped through the doorway.

The light on her face felt like an assault, at first. Her vision rapidly adjusted, but it took a moment before she could make out the figure at the far end of the hall. She was irresistibly drawn to it, her ghostly feet moving of their own accord, and slowly, details revealed themselves and mostly resolved into a tall, bronzed being with immense breadth of chest and flowing beard and hair. He? It? was dressed as her father might for a family evening at home—all leather and furs, but armorless and weaponless. A thickly-runed eyepatch obscured one eye, while the other gleamed at her from a dark face with an indescribable fierceness. The being reached his arms to her and spoke in an ocean-deep voice that resonated through her being: May I? he asked.

Aesa suddenly panicked at the thought of being engulfed by the might arrayed before her. "Um, no, thank you," she said, and rapidly cycled through panic and relief when nothing happened. The being merely lowered his arms and regarded her with a look that shocked Aesa with its familiarity; at the same time, she doubted intensely what she saw.

For that could not be fondness on his face: not fondness, and certainly not adoration for her. Not tenderness, and not welcome, and definitely not safety, for here she was, who knew how far from friends and family, and everything she knew, and this was not home, and how could her heart sing in her chest, for she had no heart to sing anymore. She wondered what would actually happen if she tried to burst into tears. Kára's eyes had seemed to well with tears, even though that hadn't made any sense at the time, and didn't make any sense now.

As she looked over the being's face her feelings threatened to swallow her whole themselves. Her sudden and terrible desire for comfort overcoming her anxiety, she flung herself forward into an embrace that seemed infinite through both time and space. She discovered, despite this, that she had not lost her sense of self; that in fact here she was, separate and herself and still her own.

She stepped back, trying to understand, and the resulting sense of loss manifested as an ache that she should not perhaps have been able to register. There were so many things about her new form that she didn't yet know. . . .

"I can feel you and not Kára," she said wonderingly, and the All-Father bewildered her again by settling down onto one of a pair of magnificently carved chairs behind him. His posture was that of a man who intended to listen intently.

Why do you think that is?

"Um," Aesa said, eloquently. She scanned his face. This wasn't a trap, or a test. There was nothing but infinite, overwhelming kindness to be read there. Why then the question, which he knew she could not accurately answer? A part of her grew cold for a moment. He was a god, and the gods could be capricious and cruel in stories. But it was so hard to be alarmed, even for a moment, in this place with its perfect, buoyant sense of well-being, in front of this entity who seemed to bear her all the good will in the world and perhaps beyond. . . .

"You and Kára are different," she hazarded, and the great eye twinkled at her.

Indeed! the being said. A little, for now. Until she grows even more into strength. For I am Óðinn, the All-Father, but someday she, and you, will reach as you did before, and clasp as you did before, even as I may reach you now.

She could not think what to say to this pronouncement. There were so many things she wanted to ask, but two questions floated through the jumble in her mind until they blocked out everything else. The questions seemed sadly petty and selfish in the face of all this grandeur: *Why did I have to die? Why didn't you help me?*

For a long, breathtakingly painful moment, Óðinn simply gazed at her, as though waiting for her to voice her questions. When she did not, he smiled like the dawn breaking over the rim of the earth. You may ask when you feel ready, he said, and she would have collapsed from relief if she could. May I introduce you to the others?

"All right," said Aesa, anxious to no longer be the sole focus of that interested scrutiny.

The All-Father rose to move past her, and flung open both of the linden doors, the handles of which he did not touch, and which seemed to tremble a little in his wake, somehow enlarging themselves for an instant into infinite space, and then decreasing again for her to walk through.

We bid welcome, he said, his voice clarion in its call. And in response, innumerable people rushed into the expanse of the hallway and crowded around each other, leaving a little space for Aesa to step into untouched, but still practically smothered in smiles and joyful waves and a sense of little wriggles as people wished to embrace, but did and could not.

These beings must be like her and Kára, despite their glorious forms and ageless faces. Off to one side, Kára herself seemed to increase in radiance just from standing among them. Many were dark-skinned like Kára. Some were even darker, and some were paler than the moon, with every shade in between, and garbed in a bewildering array of clothing. None were youthful, per se, for every person stood with the grace and confidence of maturity, but none seemed infirm in any way, and a very few faces, the ones closest to her, actually seemed familiar . . .

"*Farmor?*" she asked incredulously, her eyes trying to add the lines and whiter hair that should by rights belong to this blond and beaming lady, who laughed while clutching the hand of a similarly blond and robust man beside her. "And *Farfar*, then, too!" Aesa exclaimed, and the man nodded happily.

"I did not meet you before, but I am so glad of meeting you now," he said, his voice a resonant baritone painfully like her father's.

Aesa looked around a little at the sea of faces before daring to ask, "Father is not here? Is he . . ."

"Your father has not yet accomplished his second life, so far as we know," her grandfather confirmed, smiling. "You must speak well when he dies so he will join us here." Aesa raised an eyebrow in query, but her grandmother slugged his arm playfully.

"You know she wouldn't be sent," she said, wrinkling her nose at her husband. "And anyway she might not choose that path." She rolled her eyes at Aesa. "Even here your relations have expectations for you, yes? Don't worry, darling, we'll behave. You've so much to see, but do find us again when you wish."

"How do I do that?" Aesa asked, looking nervously at the throng of well-wishers.

Grandmother—her name had been Eygerðr, Aesa suddenly recalled—smiled gently at her, and reached up as though to brush a lock of hair from Aesa's face, before lowering her hand reluctantly. "Simply call out to me in your mind," she said, "and I'll answer."

"Probably she will," her grandfather said, "unless she's feasting."

"Or fighting," Eygerðr said. "Or three ells deep in the library. Or a hundred other things that you need to see. So go see them!" she cried, batting at Aesa's shoulders, though Aesa could not feel the blows.

"Can *she* feel it when she does that?" Aesa asked Kára, who had appeared helpfully at her elbow after her father's parents retreated into the chattering crowd. "I don't think so," Kára said thoughtfully. "The ones who can have all been here longer. Most of us still gesture out of habit anyway, because why not?"

Aesa wondered if it would be impolite to ask about the mechanics of feasting when one didn't precisely have a corporeal body. Instead, she tried her *farmor*'s instruction, and thought of the faces of her friends, trying to call to them or conjure them to her. Nothing happened, but thinking back through the conversation for hints as to why, she remembered another question she'd desperately wanted to ask.

"What did my grandfather mean about speaking well when my father dies?"

"Ah, he was likely referring to my work," Kára said. "I'd bet he's thinking you might want to serve as a valkyrja."

"So you are a valkyrja, then?" Aesa asked, glancing again over Kára's unmuscular form.

"You're wondering where my wings are, I expect," Kára replied cheerfully.

"Something like," Aesa said. "I suppose I thought you'd be a little more martial."

Kára bobbed her head. "We try to mirror your own idiom, as much as we can with integrity," she said. "You, for instance, don't seem particularly fond of weapons, despite your use of them, so I didn't wear, say, your traditional spear, shield, and sword. I thought it all might overwhelm you."

"And the other *dís*?"

"She mimics me, as best she can," Kára said, chuckling a little. "Although she sometimes does bring a rather interesting spin to it, when she thinks it'll help. Anyway, nevermind her. You're worried about your friends, and I want to help you see to them."

Aesa nodded anxiously. "Do you know yet if . . . do you have any way to find out if my friends . . . chose to come here? Or not?" She wasn't sure if she felt hopeful or terrified or both.

Her companion's face again flushed in sympathy. "We would have heard the welcome if they arrived after you, or at least you would have, if you knew them. You'll find your connection even stronger here here than it was there. But they may have made it home, or chosen Fólkvangr, despite my charming *dís* counterpart." Kára's face clouded a little. "Or . . ."

Aesa, her patience fraying, broke in. "Well, whatever the case, can we check? To see if they even died, I mean. You said before I might be able to seek them out. I could visit the fields or . . . look for their bodies, or—" She choked off, unable to continue, and Kára waited a respectful moment before answering.

"Those who choose to serve as valkyrja may travel between worlds, but . . ."

"Then I choose to be a valkyrja." The silvery feeling leapt within Aesa's chest as she spoke the words, and she nearly shrieked in frustration at the sheer randomness of its confirmations. Kára, meanwhile, just looked extremely concerned. Aesa tried to school her face into a semblance of calm patience, but she seemed to have no more control over her spirit features than she'd had in her last life.

Kára spoke cautiously, clearly weighing her words. "Aesa—I love my choice, but you don't even know what your options are yet, or about the risks involved."

"It feels like the right thing to do. That means something here, doesn't it?"

"Of course it does. But *feels* and *is* are sometimes different. You can study your choices, once I show them to you, and really make sure . . ."

Aesa shook her head fiercely. "The other *dís'* choice, Fólkvangr? It's worse than this place, isn't it. Much worse. You said so when I chose, and I've seen all those faces you've been making since. Fólkvangr is a bad place to be, isn't it."

"I'm biased," said Kára uneasily. "And we can get them out, sometimes, once they've gone in. And we don't even know if they're dead. Plus . . ."

"Right, so we should find out," Aesa broke in again. "One way or another, they're my responsibility. If they are dead, I got them killed, or you chose them to die, maybe, but the point is I need to make sure the consequences from my decisions don't keep spiraling outward and hurting everyone else."

Kára threw her head back. "Ugh, you didn't get them killed. Heimdallr's teeth, have I heard that too much. Two choices collided, and someone died. Your friends chose to be on that battlefield. If someone else swung the blade, they killed your friend. Not me, and not you."

"I led my friends to that battlefield." Aesa folded her arms across her chest.

"They chose, because of their families," Kára said, clearly trying not to roll her eyes. "I saw it. I heard it. I was there the whole battle. What good does it do you or them to claim responsibility?"

Aesa shivered angrily. "I was their leader. If I can still do something, I'm honor-bound to do it. You must understand. You chose what you did because you wanted to help, right?"

"Yes, but it's not the only way to help. Not by a long shot. I understand, I think, but you don't yet. I wouldn't be doing you a favor if I let you rush into this. Just let me show you . . ."

"Kára, I appreciate what you're offering, but I don't know if I have the patience for the grand tour right now."

"Being valkyrjur requires so much patience, though. It means biting your tongue when you would shout, and holding still when you just want to summon the strength to haul a soul straight to Ásgarðr without their permission. You saw me; I'm still not good at this, and I've been doing it for hundreds of years."

Aesa looked at the ceiling, trying again to compose her face. When she lowered her eyes, Kára looked at her anxiously but said nothing. Aesa tried to muster a smile.

"All right. I'll trust you," she said.

Kára's face lightened a little. "I know it's frustrating," she said quietly. "But I could not in good faith bring you to my chieftain before you're prepared to make an educated decision. We'll move as quickly as we can."

And so Aesa found herself half-running through a myriad spaces, driven past countless wonders by the clenched sense of urgency in her chest. Boisterous social and feasting halls quickly gave way to vaults of knowledge, with rank upon rank of heavy tomes and runestones and absorbed researchers stretching back as far as her eye could see. Under Kára's hand, the grey of one runestone changed to a light golden color, while the runes familiar to Aesa shifted into strange symbols. Aesa thought she glimpsed a bird and an eye before Kára lifted her palm, and the stone morphed back into Aesa's idiom again.

Elsewhere, under the strong light of a midday sun, Aesa watched as thousands of warriors leapt suddenly back to hale life from where they'd lain injured on one of the many practice fields of Ásgarðr—part of their daily preparation for the great battles of Ragnarök. Kára assured Aesa that Ragnarök had already essentially been won, that in fact the battles themselves would be mere formalities meant to convince their opponents of the victory, but Aesa shivered nonetheless, and they hurried on to cheery kitchens and kennels and a thousand rooms where thousands of crafters bent or crouched or huddled affectionately around a vast array of handiwork.

Near sunset, in a field dotted with a riotous variety of dwellings, Kára came to an abrupt halt before an oak-plank house so cozy and ordinary-looking that it made Aesa want to cry.

"It's a bewildering mix of familiar and unfamiliar," Kára said. "At least it was for me. So here's a home of the kind I thought you'd want, but please let me know if you'd like something else. I just didn't want to overwhelm you with even more choices."

"It's perfect," Aesa said, admiring the carving etched along the timbered eaves. She noticed that the pattern was a repeating one—the rune for protection from enemies carved over and over. Kára read the worry on Aesa's face, and spoke quickly.

"I know your houses are built to be shared, so if you get lonely, well, you know your father's parents are here, and I can make introductions to some of your ancestors."

"I've gotten used to the solitude," Aesa said truthfully, unwilling to voice her concern, and was glad when Kára did not press her further. The rune could also be read as "defense of that which one loves," which was the primary function of a house, after all. And what enemies could really roam the lands of the All-Father?

"Tomorrow, if you still want me to, I will introduce you to the chieftain of the valkyrjur," Kára said. "She'll talk you through our mission, and, ah . . ."

"Judge me worthy or not?" Aesa supplied, trying to soften her words with a smile she did not entirely feel.

Kára responded to the words and not the smile, fluttering her hands a little. "It's not about worthiness. Or even just about temperament, obviously," she said, grinning ruefully. "She'll be looking to test your resilience, and your ability to sustain compassion for others in the face of infuriating idiocy." Kára clapped her hands over her own mouth, then spoke through her fingers. "Don't tell her I said that last part, please?"

Aesa grinned despite herself. "I won't. Maybe you'll put in a good word for my discretion tomorrow, in return?"

The sound of their laughter echoed like bells across the hillside, and later, alone in a gleaming chamber, the emptiness of which for once felt like a luxury and not like a curse, Aesa discovered that for the first time in months no terrible monsters chased her through her own dreams.

Nevertheless, she was up and fully dressed when a gentle chiming sound heralded Kára's arrival at her door the next morning. Where yesterday's progress had felt like being caught up in a gale, today she had to stop herself clenching her teeth at the slowness with which Kára led her through hushed, vaulted hallways until the two arrived at yet another lindenwood portal.

CHAPTER SEVENTEEN

Beyond the door lay another vast, shadowless hall—but this one's vaults echoed with a dreadfully familiar thump-and-chime rhythm. Aesa cringed, for the sound brought to mind dozens of shame-filled afternoons spent under the impatient eye of the village weaving mistress.

"Fix," the woman would say, jabbing a finger at a near-imperceptible fault, and each scornful utterance meant half an hour of Aesa poking dismally at the weave with a tapestry needle until she'd gotten the pattern corrected to her instructor's satisfaction.

Sure enough, in the center of the hall stood a vast and improbably proportioned version of her nemesis. This loom, though, bore only a superficial resemblance to her humble version, for its shining surfaces were carved all over with runes and unnameable creatures, and the crimson threads it supported seemed to move of their own accord if Aesa looked away. Were those carvings or actual *skulls* weighting the warp at the bottom?

A solitary woman moved from behind the loom as Kára and Aesa approached, turning a calm but unsmiling face towards her visitors.

Her dark eyes looked friendly, though, in an intimidating sort of way, and she extended her hands in apparent welcome.

"Aesa, this is Herja, my chieftain," Kára said, ushering Aesa forward. "Herja, Aesa."

"You wish to know more about the valkyrjur," Herja stated in a deep and mellow contralto.

"I wish to be a valkyrja," Aesa said firmly.

Herja inclined her head in acknowledgement. "What do you know about us?"

Aesa shuffled a bit. "What I've been taught, mostly, about the women who choose those who will fall in battle. And bits I've heard in songs and stories, about ravens and swans and riding fierce horses back to Ásgarðr, although none of that seems to have been borne out so far." She glanced over Herja's shoulder at the vast bulk of the gleaming loom. "Um, I'm not great at weaving, but I'm willing to learn and practice if someone will teach me . . ."

She trailed off and shrugged, embarrassed. Despite Kára's assurances that the anxiety would fade, she did not enjoy the sense of backward ignorance she felt in the presence of . . . well, nearly everyone here. Herja evidently read the discomfort on Aesa's face, for she grimaced sympathetically.

"I'm not asking to ridicule you," she said. "I need to know what misconceptions you might have. I would treat you as a blank slate, but you aren't. You already have ideas about what the valkyrjur do, and I don't want you to be disappointed down the road when you find out that those ideas were not based on fact. For instance, the valkyrjur do not choose who dies in battle."

Hearing the statement felt like an enormous blow to Aesa's chest. Some part of her, she realized now, had been silently, desperately hoping that piece of lore was true—that violent deaths made sense, that they had meaning, that they in fact brought honor because to be chosen by the gods to die in battle meant one was worthy and good. The idea had brought order and peace to her life, in a way, and here that peace had been stripped from her in an instant.

Although Kára and Herja were giving her space to process the revelation, something in her still wanted to snarl at the messenger who had delivered the blow, and she began to understand why someone might choose to leave this place, with its unflinching truth tellers, and retreat towards a hope of a less-demanding welcome in Fólkvangr.

"But—*valkyrja* means 'chooser of the slain,' right?" she said carefully. "I don't quite understand why you're still using the title if it doesn't, well, apply."

Kára winced a little, but Herja's eyes went soft.

"It's the closest concept in your language to what we are," she said. "There's just a little bit of historical confusion about our purpose. One of our tasks is to proffer transport to Valhǫll for those we think might do well here. In practical reality, that means offering the option to everyone we can. While the All-Father has granted us the right of judicious selection, we've largely discovered that our external judgment of someone's character is not as accurate as their own assessment. And the real choice, you will no doubt discover, is not just to come here, but to remain."

Aesa tried to disguise her dismay, but the news came as another blow to her ego—dispelling the notion that she'd been selected because she was somehow special and worth the attention of not one, but two *dísir*.

Kára must have seen the disappointment on Aesa's face, for she rushed through her next words. "I think . . . I hope you'll come to see that your worth to us is infinite. I've observed you, and I hope with time you'll feel known, not just by me, but everyone here. Because if you feel known, you might also understand how much it would hurt me to lose you again, now that you're here." She clenched her fists a little and looked beseechingly at Herja, who reached out her hand and briefly clasped the other woman's. Apparently comforted, Kára tried again.

"I'm not telling you this to make you feel guilty. It's that like I said before, I want you to understand. Being valkyrja comes with a lot of power to act, but it can also mean feeling a lot of sadness, and a lot of frustration. Our only good weapons in the fight for souls are truth and kindness, and there have been many days when those weapons just don't feel mighty enough."

She glanced briefly at Herja, but there was no censure on the other woman's face. Herja was intent on Aesa, who flushed under the scrutiny.

"Um," Aesa said into the silence, "Hanging up my weapons sounds all right to me. And I know how to bite my tongue when it's necessary. I'm even decent at it, most of the time. I can only imagine I'll get better with practice."

"Willingness counts for a lot here," Herja said, inclining her head. "Another thing to know is that you'd work with a kind of support team. They'll check in with you about your mental and spiritual health."

"How?" Aesa said, taken aback.

"Talking, mostly," Herja said. "Your team will consult with you and with each other about how you're doing, and it will take a lot of honesty from you."

"Because being a valkyrja can make you sad?" Aesa asked, trying to shake off a wave of revulsion at the thought of someone trying to poke around her emotional innards. "I've been sad. I can handle sad," she said.

"I don't doubt it," Herja said. "Nevertheless, this is an essential part of your duties. There's sad and then there's *sad*, and it's our job to keep you in good form."

Her words made Aesa recall the sight of one of her formerly joyful aunts, immobile with grief in a darkened house under a pile of blankets despite the heat of summer, and she shuddered. She didn't want to be leveled like that, and she did not yet trust these strangers with her feelings. "What if I refuse?"

"You aren't given an assignment," Herja said with a slight shrug. "Everyone on an active duty of any kind is required to meet with their support team. You think being slaughtered every day before lunch is easy on the soul?"

"It certainly isn't easy on the stomach, blecch," Kára added, shuddering.

"Your support team is highly trained, and they'll focus on what you want to address," Herja said. "The team makes adjustments around you until it's a positive experience."

Aesa brought Dotta's face to her mind, trying to draw strength from thinking of her. "I'd give it a try, I guess," she said. "What else do I need to know?"

Herja regarded her for a long moment. "A lot," she admitted, "but I know you're anxious to see to your friends, and I imagine you'd agree to nearly anything to help them. I don't want that for you, so I'm willing to grant you the powers of the valkyrjur, and let you decide later if it's the way you really want to serve." Kára glanced at Herja's face, clearly concerned, which made Aesa nervous.

"I'm not . . . I mean, I'm not just agreeing with everything to get what I want," she said. Herja gazed at her placidly, but Kára raised a worried and skeptical eyebrow.

"Well, not much," Aesa amended. "Being a valkyrja really does sound like what I'd most like to do. It's just a lot to adapt to. Kára's tried to tell me so, but I guess it's just now sinking in." She made an apologetic face at Kára, who promptly stuck her tongue out, then smiled.

Herja coughed politely. "I understand. That's why I'll let you give it a try, as you say. Please don't worry; you'll have as many tries as you'd like. But know that I'm concerned about the way you approach things now. I'm afraid your intensity will wear you out quickly when it's not your loved ones you're helping, but strangers."

The words stung. "I can care about strangers," Aesa said, doing her best to keep her tone even.

"I believe you," Herja said. "But a shared history often lends us a resiliency we might not be able to muster when helping someone we don't know. To combat that, we ask for help, from our teams, from each other, and, failing all else, from the gods directly. You don't seem well-prepared to ask for or receive help. Perhaps you haven't had access, or your help hasn't been reliable."

"I ask for help all the time. I even ask the gods for help all the time."

"But do you actually expect that you'll receive it?"

Aesa started to nod, but as she watched Herja's face for signs of belief, something tore loose, and she flung her arms out, exasperated.

"I mean, all right, why would I? I've asked for help and gotten it, sometimes, when people can give it, but so often they can't. I won't fault them for that. And the gods—well, of course I've asked. We're taught it's insulting if we don't. But I haven't exactly seen results, not even when it really, really mattered."

She lifted her chin defiantly, prepared for censure, but Herja simply gazed back with eyes full of sympathy. Somehow made even more furious by this woman's calm acceptance of everything, Aesa looked away. "Just tell me what help I can ask for and reliably get. There must be some kind of a list, or something."

"Here, you may ask for anything you like, and you will receive it, in time," Herja said.

Quickly, Kára added, "Just, ah, make sure you're asking for what you really want, and not what you think you can get."

"Fine," said Aesa. "I want to get out of here and check on my friends. Please give me the power to do so."

"May I touch you?" Herja asked.

Aesa shrugged her acceptance. Herja smiled minutely before she stepped uncomfortably close in order to reach a hand to the back of Aesa's skull. Aesa did in fact feel this, somehow—a pressure and warmth and a sense of affection that mixed itself into the roiling confusion and resentment and hope in her stomach.

There were words that Herja spoke to her, clearly ritualistic, but Aesa found her mind unwilling to focus on the gentle murmur, so anxious was she to get this over with and finally go. She found herself surprised, therefore, when the pressure on the back of her neck eased not long after it began.

Aesa surreptitiously checked herself over. She didn't feel any different, really. Perhaps there was more of a sense of Herja and Kára's presences in the room, as though their persons were somehow a little larger than their own bodies, now. She looked up to see Herja walking away.

"Come back when you've achieved your aims, and we'll get you an assignment," Herja said over her shoulder.

"That's it?" a skeptical Aesa asked. A sudden fear washed through her. Had she missed something through her inattention? "I don't swear an oath of fealty or anything?"

"Your oath is in your actions," Herja said before giving a little wave and leaving through an anteroom door.

Half-amazed, Aesa turned to Kára, who shrugged and grinned at her. "What's the use of swearing to do good? Just do it," she said happily. "Unless you'd like more ceremony—I'm sure we could put something together."

"Thank you, no," Aesa said, shaking her head. "But, uh, speaking of doing good . . . well, this may be awkward, but you mentioned, um, powers?"

Kára's smile widened. "Yes! You'll find you have some now. I wish I could tell you more, but it's really different for everyone. We can all move between Ásgarðr and Miðgarðr, I think. Beyond that, we mostly figure it out as we go."

"Heading back to Miðgarðr sounds good," Aesa said, trying not to sound too anxious about it.

"Come on, then, I'll show you a good starting place."

After a brief journey through glimmering corridors and half-wild gardens, Aesa found herself approaching a granite platform set into a break in a towering wall. Helmed figures ensconced in guardposts scanned the skies, but Kára ignored them entirely and drew Aesa to the center of an intricate pattern etched into the rock. The wall seemed to sit right at the edge of a cliff, for past the platform, Aesa could see nothing but sky.

"Why didn't we arrive here?" she asked.

"It's mostly a practice space. Some people don't enjoy heights much," Kára said, gesturing toward the cliff edge, which was admittedly far too near for Aesa's liking. The clouds suspended in the dazzling blue felt much closer than they ought, and Aesa hadn't seen a single bird since she'd arrived.

"By way of training, I'm going to have you take us down to

Miðgarðr, so you can overcome any fear of it right away," Kára told her. "Just sort of think 'down.'"

"Wait, I'm just going to *what*? Shouldn't I—I don't know—practice first?"

Kára's face scrunched sympathetically. "There's not really a way to practice other than doing, I'm afraid. I'll catch you if it becomes too much. But I expect you'll do fine."

Aesa wrinkled her nose, but took a deep breath and closed her eyes to concentrate. *Down*, she thought, half-hoping nothing would happen. Nothing did happen at first, but as she tried harder to picture herself sinking, she slowly realized that she actually was. When she opened her eyes again, she discovered that the granite platform was now in fact above her, and that the next-closest ground was thousands of feet away. Her stomach tried to revolt and her feet uselessly beat the air.

Kára drifted gently down beside her, reaching out to carefully clasp her by the arms. "Murp," Aesa declared plaintively. Kára pursed her lips as though to stifle a giggle.

"You're doing great," she said. "Just keep thinking 'down.'"

They descended with a terrible sort of slowness. Aesa tried to reduce her panic by observing the tops of the mountains as they approached, and even tried a bit of experimental maneuvering. The sight of an eagle soaring far below made her flinch, but her progress by now seemed inexorable, and they did not stop.

"What happens if we hit it?" Aesa said, gesturing at the wheeling eagle. Seeing a bird of prey from the wrong side was for some reason unnerving to her in a way nothing else had been so far.

"We can't hit it," Kára replied mildly. "We don't really occupy the same space as mortal things. I've been trying to learn how it works, but there's a lot to understand, so none of it really makes sense to me yet. Oh, and until you grow in power, no one will be able to see you, for better or for worse."

When at last they reached the upper platform's twin, solidly embedded into the cool, greening earth, Aesa thought for a moment of flinging herself down onto it, then glanced at Kára and resisted the urge. She supposed she ought to maintain her dignity among other valkyrjur until she knew more about how things were done.

"Your town is an easy journey that way," Kára said, pointing west. "You can make it more quickly if you can bring yourself to move in the space between things, but it made me sick the first few times I tried it. Would you like me to come with you?"

The longing to fling herself on the ground had not dissipated, and more importantly, she knew that she wanted to keep private the emotions she might feel upon discovering the fate of her friends. She didn't want to seem ungrateful for the offer, though. Aesa looked a little unhappily at Kára, but decided that telling the truth was the best course of action.

"I know I ought to say yes, especially given the speech Herja made about asking for help, but . . ."

"Say no more," Kára said, her hands up. "I won't take a new assignment until I know you're all right, so just call to me if you want me, and I'll come quick as blinking. Don't worry: I move a little faster than you do at the moment."

She winked and waved a cheery goodbye. Then there was a rather dazzling flash of light, and Kára was gone, leaving afterimages dancing in Aesa's vision.

After giving her head a good shake, Aesa glanced around, then hurled herself onto the welcoming and familiar ground. She could not feel the grass prickling her cheek or the chilly mud beneath her, but her heart still thrilled to see the sky and the clouds in their correct distances and proportions, with the birds winging above her where they properly belonged.

CHAPTER EIGHTEEN

ONCE AESA PICKED HERSELF BACK UP AGAIN, she discovered that the business of getting around quickly was not as simple as descending from Ásgarðr had made it seem. While she could move at her normal walking pace, and even sort of sprint for brief bursts, she realized that she'd assumed travelling would be much more rapid as a valkyrja, given how she and Kára had reached Ásgarðr almost instantaneously that first time. The trick of "think down" did not seem to apply to "think forward," or "think faster."

For a while she was furious at Kára for not helping her get closer to her destination, and for a while after that she was furious at herself for letting Kára leave right away. She did try walking through the trees that stood between her and a straight-line path home, but learned that passing through objects was indeed incredibly disorienting, and she grumpily gave up, since it took her so long to recover after making it through one sapling that there seemed to be no actual gains to her progress.

She thought about calling Kára back, but decided that having to say, "Thank you for the help; now please go away again," would be hard on both of their dignities.

She felt fairly tireless, though, which was nice, and suddenly essential, when she realized that she was probably on the back side of one of the mountains that surrounded her village. Since the mountain itself was part of a long chain, the fastest way home would be over, or through. She squared her shoulders, and placed her hands against one dusty hill before willing herself to march through. She even got a few feet in to the dark, strange space before a sense of claustrophobia and suffocation overwhelmed her, sending her scurrying back for the light. "You don't even breathe!" she told herself, but settled on trying to scale the face instead of walk through it. She happily realized, a third of the way up, that she was getting stronger, that her steps were now more like bounds up the craggy mountainside, and that she fairly darted from one incline to another, as though she were more goat than person.

By the time she reached the summit, she was able to skip steps all together, moving instead in little leaps. She half wished it were sunrise, for viewing the valley at daybreak had always been one of her secret dreams. As it was, the vista before her still almost pained her with its beauty, especially because from this height, amidst the sunset-painted patchwork of farms and dusty paths and hills and stubborn brush trees, she could see the homes of everyone she held most dear—even Martyn and Cynisca's little steading far down the coast.

She rushed down the mountainside, past the start of the treeline, past the barrow mounds where many of her ancestors had been interred, past the cave where she and Kiaran and Ingirun had huddled as they watched the *møtehall* burn . . . and then stopped abruptly as she noticed the neat line of boats that had been pulled up onto the shore of their cove. An attempt had been made to rebuild around the remnants of the *møtehall*, and from within its patchy walls came the sound of a terribly familiar voice . . .

Aesa crept close, and put her eye to a gap in one of the slats, before remembering that she did not have to hide. She steeled herself before *pushing* directly through the tanned hide serving for a door, and found herself almost immediately shivering in the tension that flooded her mind from dozens of sources as she entered the space.

Torches had already been lit inside, despite the fact that it was not yet twilight, and the fiery glow flickered on a number of grim faces. Kiaran stood in the center of the room, half shouting at a man she recognized one of her father's extended troop, who sat in a chair elevated on a rude platform set against one wall. Mette leaned against another wall as near as she could get to Kiaran, her expression stony. Nefja, Geirny, Dotta, and several others from Aesa's warband huddled in a corner, while between them more of her father's compatriots lined the other walls, or crouched where there was not space to stand. Fear radiated from them in dull greenish waves, and Aesa had to push down a sense of sympathetic nausea in order to hear what was being said.

"What evidence do you have to prove these accusations?" the seated man—Aesa thought his name might be Berinhart—was asking Kiaran.

"Plenty, if those involved will but be brave enough to confess," Kiaran said, gesturing around the room. "Or if they are cowardly, then the absence of those who would be here except for their foolishness. Your own captain's daughter, whom I loved deeply, is not here with us because these unnatural women led her to her death."

"Many faces are lately missing from among our ranks," Berinhart said calmly. "My own brother is absent from his hearth, as are my uncles." He turned his gaze upon the women clumped in the corner. "Do you wish to confess to taking up arms?" he asked, plainly amused by his own question.

"It's ridiculous to even ask," said Nefja's brother Magnus hotly as he pushed past a burly man resplendent in silver armbands. Aesa's view of Magnus was overlaid by a sort of purple tinge at the edges of her vision, and she blinked and shook her head, trying to clear it.

"Do these look like bloodthirsty woman-warriors to you?" Magnus asked, sweeping his arm towards Aesa's friends. "Dotta there couldn't harm anything if her own father begged her to. And everyone knows Geirny can barely stand to have an animal slaughtered, let alone a person."

"Ridiculous?" Kiaran sneered, and Aesa blinked again, for where Magnus had gleamed violet, Kiaran seemed to show no color at all.

"Ridiculous is letting yourself be captured, then rescued by your own sister," Kiaran continued. "You should be ashamed to still name yourself member of our clan, let alone helping them cover up their crimes now."

"It is not yet official law that a woman should not take up arms," Berinhart said. "If what you say is true, these women did a brave thing. Why does this anger you so, Kiaran Vigison?"

"They pollute our ways and bring suffering to the small and weak-minded," Kiaran said promptly. "Who knows how they pressured others into seeking out danger? I myself tried to stop them, and they rejected my counsel and cast aside those who would have set a better example. Mette, for instance, found herself friendless and alone when she refused to participate in their foolish schemes."

Mette did her best to look downcast, but landed mostly on sulky petulance. Aesa did not think those watching appreciated the difference, though Mette's internal struggle displayed itself to Aesa like a flicker of color ranges. A man standing near Mette reached out to pat her arm comfortingly, and she simpered at him briefly before fixing her eyes on Kiaran again.

"It does you credit that you champion the weak," Berinhart said to Kiaran, "but I do not yet see how it is a matter for the law. I cannot order these women to befriend Mette."

There was a cough from further back along the room, and a dark-haired man stepped forward. "You are not a father of daughters, Berinhart, so perhaps you cannot understand as one so honored might," he said. "But I find myself greatly saddened at the thought of my precious girl facing danger and blood. We are happy to serve as their defenders, for that is our role, and in return, I expect my child to live so she can fulfill hers. I want this unwomanly attitude quashed here, if anything like what Kiaran describes happened."

Aesa began to feel something like a headache coming on, as though a swarm of angry bees was clustering at the top of her skull.

Another man cleared his throat. "I'm not so good at speaking as Tvæggi here," he said, "but I want to say I agree, somewhat. Things here work because my girls help their mam, and my strong-armed boys help me protect them. My boys are better at shoving the plow, and my girls will be better at shoving out babies."

He acknowledged the chuckles that filled the room before continuing. "If these women went out fighting, then all right, things were bad, but they need to see sense and settle down again so things can continue as they ought. Once a woman gets combative, it spills out into your home life, see? And that's bad for the whole village."

The man flushed brightly as he finished, but several men clapped him about the shoulders while he stepped back into his former place.

"He knows of what he speaks," one of the back-slappers remarked. "I've heard his wife squeaking and squawking at him when he just wants a rest. I'm surprised he hasn't backhanded her afore now."

A few more phantom bees joined the swarm of Aesa's anger.

Berinhart leaned on his elbow, his mouth twitching.

"Well, then," he said solemnly. "The way forward seems clear."

He looked to the corner where Aesa's friends clustered, catching each gaze in turn. Dotta looked steadfastly at the floor in refusal, but Berinhart seemed unfazed.

"Girls, I am moved by your modesty and your silence. Given the absence of our highest chieftain, I shall protect you as he no doubt would." His smile included all the men in the room, and they began to smile in response.

"We will not expose you and your families to shame by forcing you to confess if you did in fact take up arms. In return, these men would ask you to lay them down again, and return to your peaceful arts and learning. Is this acceptable to you?"

The mens' smiles were broad now. Berinhart leaned forward, proffering his hand.

"No," Geirny said clearly.

Berinhart sat back amid a rumble of surprise and anger. Kiaran looked smugly incredulous, and Aesa longed for corporeal form so she could do . . . *something* about it. The buzzing in the back of her mind reached a fever pitch.

Geirny stepped forward into the middle of the room. Ignoring Kiaran, she held her hands out to the other warriors.

"You were handpicked by Ottar Þorfiðrson himself, so I know you are mighty and valorous. But you are also few," she said sternly. "Our village is still at risk from those who would take our lands for themselves. We hold one such would-be conqueror captive now, and there will no doubt be others who follow him. We are not so well trained as you," she said, somehow not catching Kiaran's eye, "nor have we much experience yet, but if we women join you, then we have enough for an army of the size that can repulse an enemy from our shores."

Aesa began to panic, for only Nefja's brother looked pleased. The other men ranged from surprised to angry, and Kiaran was near hysterical with triumph.

"You see?" he said, flinging his arm toward Geirny. "These unnatural women betray every tradition we hold sacred."

"Tradition doesn't make something right," cried Dotta, wrestling her way up to Geirny. She glared up at Kiaran. "I know you like tradition because you benefit from it, and that makes you angry about change. But change is here, so you might as well quit yelling about it and help us. Help us more, in fact. Did you know he trained us?" she said, turning to face the rest of the men in the room. "He's trying to sell us out now, but he was all for us before."

"I thought I could keep you from hurting yourselves," Kiaran snarled back. "And it's not simply tradition you pervert here. Will you really offend the gods by rejecting their special gifts to you?"

"How do you know the gods don't want us armed?" Nefja said angrily, but Berinhart stomped his feet on the platform until Dotta clapped her hands to her ears.

The sight stirred the energy in Aesa's head until her sense of it became near-tangible. She pushed experimentally at the energy, trying to direct it somehow towards the heated iron sensation she had of Berinhart's mind. Her first attempts moved it not at all, and she redoubled her efforts, but the energy did not budge.

"We will have order," Berinhart roared, breaking her focus. "You women are not generally present at councils, so you do not know how things are done. Now," he continued in a calmer tone, shaking his head. "Kiaran, you know well that the gods care about our sacrifices, and our honor, but the business of men they leave to men to adjudicate."

Kiaran kept his mouth shut, vibrating with fury. Berinhart acknowledged his frustration, extending his hands in a conciliatory half shrug. "In the absence of Ottar Þorfiðrson, I am most senior. He trusts me to decide, and I shall decide."

Grim-faced, he again slowly looked over the women huddled together behind Geirny. Before he could speak, Aesa frantically reversed course. She stopped trying to *push* the energy from her own mind, but instead used it to *pull* at the reddish-grey sparking around Berinhart's edges.

She yanked too hard in her fright, causing Berinhart to suddenly clutch at his head.

Aesa loosed her grip immediately and shuddered at the pain she'd felt along their connection. Berinhart seemed to be recovering, but sat rubbing his temple and blinking in evident stupefication.

Aesa thought quickly, and this time, as best as she could, gently crooked a mental finger in a sort of invitation.

Something shifted in Berinhart's expression. She felt his mind respond in a sort of curious yellow that she took to mean acceptance. She pulled again, a little more strongly than last time, trying to thread his consciousness into her memories. She tried to show him images of angry Skjöldungar and acquisitive Ylfling. She twined his thoughts around her recollections of her warband, doing their best to train and prepare like any other Bjǫrn warriors.

Through their connection, Aesa sensed Berinhart's distress as he encountered ideas that conflicted so much with his opinions about the natural order of things. She felt for him, but redoubled her efforts nonetheless. He pushed back. Aesa scrambled for even more powerful images to soothe his concerns. She showed him Dotta's actions on the battlefield, and Sigrun's, and Nefja's, and Geirny's—

their bravery and determination shining from their faces like beacons at midnight.

Their connection began to slip. Although Aesa had only held Berinhart's attention for a few seconds, she realized that she was quickly coming to the end of her strength, and she reluctantly released his mind. She found that her power was now too spent to even see the faintest colors of his thoughts.

So instead Aesa searched his face, just as she would have as a mortal, hoping for a sign that she'd shown him enough to quell his fear and fury. She could discern little for a long moment. *Please, All-Father,* she thought. *Please let me have done this right.* The silvery feeling, stronger than ever, leapt joyfully in her chest, and she would have collapsed for the relief of it.

But Berinhart's gaze, liquid and dark, still flicked over the room at length, as though measuring the strength of each individual occupant. At last he settled back against the elaborate carvings of his chair and spoke.

"Geirny Róghvatrsdóttir: if matters stand as you say, then we may indeed require the aid of all who are willing in order to defend ourselves," he said slowly. "I will see to your captive, and if I am satisfied, then you women shall join our ranks and be trained as our young men would be."

There were several roars of dismay, but he quelled them with a shake of his head.

"It has been done in other places," he said sternly. "We would be unwise to turn down this offer of aid while so many of our best are still afield. When our ranks are again swelled, we may reconsider, but for now, my decision is made."

Aesa noticed several men look at Geirny with dislike, but she was distracted by Kiaran's next words.

"I do not agree that the gods will be so mild in their feelings about what has taken place here," Kiaran said, looking balefully about. "If this is your decision, then I, for one, will exert my rights to take my household and find other company to fight alongside."

Mette blanched and grabbed his arm. "Kiaran—your farm . . . your mother . . ." she said, clearly seeing her dreams of wealth and governance slipping away from her.

He shook her off impatiently. "I must do what is right, no matter the cost. I cannot live among those who would endanger such gentle creatures as yourself." He wheeled on the other warriors again. "You're all cowards, you know," he spat. "Cowards who would hide behind women's bodies in battle. I trained them myself; they won't stand against an onslaught."

"We did, though." Nefja's voice, furious and shaking but mostly controlled, piped high over Kiaran's outraged tenor. "We faced battle, and we most of us lived. We are blooded, and we have proved ourselves."

"Most lived," Kiaran repeated, his lip curling. "Most, but not all. Women died where no women need have died. Women who could have brought literal life to this village. A woman I could have loved, and your foolishness took her from me. I cannot stay where her memory haunts me. Will anyone else have the courage to stand for what is right?"

He looked hard into the faces of the other young men in the room. Some looked away, but only a pair of men stirred from where they stood. Kiaran's face mottled with anger and he strode for the doorway, his two friends hurrying awkwardly behind. "Cowards all!" he roared on his way out, but did not turn, and no one else followed.

"Well," said Berinhart as the door-skin fell back into place. "We should commend you ladies, I suppose. Now that your actions are out in the open, I may say that your bravery in retrieving our captured kinsfolk brings much honor to you." Nefja grinned, and her brother stepped to her and saluted before embracing her, mostly dissipating the remaining tension.

Geirny signaled, and the women formed up behind her in a double row to leave. Outside and up the hill a little ways, though, they let their ranks dissolve into a joyful huddle instead, and they all exploded into a high-pitched chatter, their voices swelled by relief.

Aesa's heart nearly broke from having to watch them instead of joining in. She settled for sort of cuddling into the outside edge of the group, and when the lateness of the hour at last sent reluctant feet trudging towards sleep, Aesa hung back with Geirny, to serve as an invisible companion on the long, dark walk home.

In the dimness, she thought about trying to communicate. She could try to let Geirny know that she was all right, and that there was life of a strange sort after death, and so much of their fear about it was needless. But as she gazed at her friend's dear face, she gave in to the sad sense that it wouldn't be the right thing to do. Geirny had little enough privacy at home in a house stuffed in the traditional way with family and servants and sometimes even livestock. She didn't need to know that the spirits of the dead could observe her at will without her permission, and although she had not been officially instructed, Kára had told her that they were honor-bound not to try to give away too much about the afterlife.

But because she was there by Geirny's side, she was able to notice movement in the night's stillness, and the faint glint of moonlight from a bared blade. Stealthy and intent, Kiaran's long legs ate up the distance on the slope between himself and his prey. His blade flashed out, and Aesa, whose hands grabbed uselessly at his arms, let out a great shout that tore through the silence. *NO!*

Kiaran staggered back, dropping his dagger to clutch at his head, and Geirny looked around wildly before snatching up the dagger and sprinting for the light of the closest dwelling. Kiaran shook his head angrily, and tried to stumble after her, but Geirny pounded on the door and Aesa hissed in his ear, *Run, fiend.*

She was not certain if he'd heard her, for at that moment the house door was flung open, and Geirny was pulled inside by the welcoming arms of Dotta's family. Kiaran did run, then, sprinting back into the underbrush along the pathway, and Aesa did not follow, for the thought of pursuing him pained her heart somehow, and armed men and women were already spilling out from Dotta's house to give chase.

Aesa hurried toward Geirny, hoping to perhaps bring comfort with her presence, somehow. As she looked in through the doorway, though, and witnessed her friend embraced by warm, solid arms, a sharp pain tore through her. She had expected to simply be glad for Geirny's safety, but instead, in the cheery glow of the open doorway she felt an unwelcome, overwhelming grief for the world to which she no longer belonged.

Not just grief. Anxiety roiled in her heart about the future, and her absent family. Aesa even discovered that some part of her still half-expected someone to chastise her for shouting at Kiaran. Unmarried women did not shout, after all. It was unkind. It was stupid. And yet she had helped save Geirny's life by shouting at the man her heart had once longed for.

Aesa shook her head as she took one last look. For nearly her entire life, some part of her had been so certain she'd marry Kiaran. She'd been sure that their destinies were intertwined like threads on the loom of fate. But she'd just watched him disappear into

ACKNOWLEDGEMENTS

It takes a village to complete any major undertaking, and this work is no exception. I owe debts of gratitude to so many for their help, witting or not, with this book. To Megan Lally, for her discerning eye and her enthusiasm. To Dr. Nola Smith, for reading my terrible first drafts, and to Dr. Zena Hassan, for inspiring them. To Ronda Eady, Dr. Tausif Muzaffar, Helen Silverstein, Monica Steeves, and Parley Smith for patiently reading development drafts. To Rosalyn Helps, for weighing in. To Louise DuCray-Medley, for a precious loan. To Dr. Zofia Wilamowska, for her wisdom. And to my beloved husband, for making this possible.

AESA OTTARSDÓTTIR: /æˈsɑː ˈʊtɑrʃdutɪr/
BJORN: /ˈbjʊrn/
CYNISCA: /sɪˈnɪskə/
DOTTA: /ˈdʊtɑ/
FREDERIKKE: /frɛdɛrˈɪkə/
GEIRNY RÓGHVATRSDÓTTIR: /ˈgɛɪrny ˈrʊgvɑtrʃdutɪr/
GNORRI: /ˈgnʊri/
GNUPA: /ˈgnʉpɑː/
HERJA: /ˈhɛrjɑː/
INGIRUN: /ˈinjirʉn/
JÓFREIÐR: /jʊfˈreðr/
KÁRA /ˈkɑʊːrɑː/
KIARAN: /kiˈɑrɑn/
MARTYN: /ˈmɑrtyn/
MAGNUS: /ˈmɑgnʉs/
NEFJA: /ˈnefjɑ/
NIDBIORG: /ˈnɪdbiʊrg/
ØRLYGR: /ˈørlygr/
PANUK: /ˈpɑnʉk/
PORSI: /ˈpʊrʃi/
PUTUGUQ: /ˈpʉtʉgʉk/
RODMAR: /ˈrʊdmɑr/
SIGRUN: /ˈsɪgrʉn/
SKJÖLDUNGAR: /ˈsçœːldəngɑr/
SVENI: /ˈsven-i/
VIGI ULFRIKSON: /ˈvigi ˈʉlfriksun/
YLFING: /ˈylfing/

GLOSSARY

Berserker: /bə(ɹ)ˈzɜː(ɹ)kəɾ/ A warrior-shaman dressed in a ritual costume made from the hide of a bear. The costume was a visual indicator that the wearer had temporarily forsaken his humanity and become a divine predator.

Dís: /ˈdiːs/ A female spirit, possibly a goddess

Dísir: /ˈdiːsiɾ/ The plural of dís

Eir: /ˈeiɾ/ A spirit or goddess of mercy and healing, possibly with life-giving or life-taking powers

Elli: /ˈelli/ A giantess who is the personification of old age

Eostre: /ˈeustɾe/ A spirit or goddess of fertility and the dawn

Farfar: /ˈfɑrfɑr/ Paternal grandfather

Farmor: /ˈfɑrmɔr/ Paternal grandmother

Freyja: /ˈfreiə/ A goddess-sorceress, Freyja can use divination to forsee the outcome of a plan of action

Fylgia: /ˈfʏljɑ/ A guardian spirit, generally taking an animal form, which accompanies a person on their life journey.

Heimdallr: /ˈheimˌdaːlr/ A golden-toothed god credited with the creation of the social class system

Hermóðr: /ˈhɛrmuð̩r/ A son and occasional page of Óðinn's, Hermóðr was famously single-minded about his pursuits

Jarl: /jaːl/ Belonging to the first free caste; chieftains

Jarlar: /ˈjaːlɑr/ Plural of jarl

Karl: /kaːl/ Belonging to the second free caste

Karlar: /ˈkaːlɑr/ Plural of karl

Møte: /ˈmøːtə/ A meeting

Nanna: /ˈnænə/ A goddess of empowerment

Óðinn: /ˈoðin/ Aesa's primary patron god

Ragnarök: /ˈrɑːɡnəˌrɒk/ An as-yet-unfought battle prophesied of by seers, in which many gods are destined to perish

Reinsdyrstek: /ˈræɪnsˌdyːrstek/ A special-occasion dish consisting of roasted reindeer meat

Shaman: /ˈʃeɪmən/ A practicioner of destiny magic

Skraeling: /ˈskræːliŋɡ/ A pejorative term for a native of Greenland

Solidus: /ˈsɒlɪdəs/ A gold coin used in the late Roman Empire

Sǫfjn: /ˈsʊfjn/ A goddess of relationships

Thrall: /ˈθræl/ Belonging to the third, or slave caste.

Týr: /ˈtɪr/ A war god known as a guarantor of oaths

Þing: /ˈθɪŋ/ A political assembly, held at the new or full moon

Þórr: /ˈθɔɹ/ A war god who favors brute force

Valhǫll: /ˈval.hɒlː/ The halls of the dead presided over by Óðinn.

Valkyrja: /ˈvælˌkɪˌɹja/ Old Norse for valkyrie

Valkyrjur: /ˈvælˌkɪˌɹjʉr/ The plural of VALKYRJA

Var: /ˈvaɾ/ A goddess of contracts and oaths